Spring Blues

A UFC ROMANTIC COMEDY

BLAIR MONROY

Books by Blair Monroy

GIRL FIGHT SERIES

Girl Fight

Spring Blues

Summer Storm

Autumn Falling

Cover

Title

Copyright

Books by

Dedication

Contents

Playlist

Playlist

EVA'S

THE BOY IS MINE | ARIANA GRANDE

JEALOUS | NICK JONAS

SWEET NOTHING | TAYLOR SWIFT

SAD GIRL | LANA DEL REY

PRETTY PLEASE | DUA LIPA

STILL INTO YOU | PARAMORE

JEALOUSY JEALOUSY | OLIVIA RODRIGO

ERIC'S

SOMEDAY YOU WILL BE LOVED | DEATH CAB FOR CUTIE

I WILL WAIT | MUMFORD AND SONS

KEEP ON TRUCKIN' | TIM MCGRAW

UNBREAK MY HEART | TONI BRAXTON

HAVANA | CAMILA CABELLO

MAKEOUT POINT | THE FRIGHTS

MELTING | CUCO

To my amazing ARC Team. I couldn't have done it without you.

CHAPTER

ONE

SPRING HIT THE VALLEY like a midlife crisis—sudden, sweaty, and relentless. By noon, the heat had already sent three tourists to the ER with quick onset dehydration, the heat so intense they reportedly tried to drink the Venetian gondola water. *Eww.*

It came like a tornado, but instead of wind, heat.

That's Vegas, baby.

All neon glitter and bottomless mimosas until you remember it's built on a desert that's basically Satan's personal sauna. (Or, if you're Felicia-level crude, Satan's asshole.)

Survival tip 101: SPF 100 and a therapist on speed dial.

And a hydration pack?

I slumped in my car—a gaudy green thing with the personality of a depressed tortoise—debating whether to suffocate in stale AC or roast like a rotisserie chicken. The fresh air option was a joke. Opening the window felt like sticking my face in a hair dryer set to vengeance.

My phone buzzed, Felicia texting she was "omw!!"

(Translation: "I haven't left the café yet and I've just remembered I have to bake a batch of muffins. Sorry!")

I groaned. Felicia's "omw" was less a promise and more a threat. Last week, "omw" meant she was meant to leave on time, but you see, Shane didn't know how to operate the La Marzocco and she had to teach him, and could I be a dear and wait an hour? Maybe two. Today? I'd be lucky if she arrived before the asphalt melted.

The heat shimmered off the parking lot, warping the Strip's skyline into a Dali painting. I missed winter. Those crisp mornings when my breath fogged the air and my bad decisions felt… cooler. *Next year*, I vowed, *I'll appreciate snowflakes instead of grumping through them like disgruntled sour grapes.*

Lies. All lies.

Spring had arrived with its heat and color, and my life was stuck in B&W. It wasn't just bleak. Bleak was too kind. Bleak implied a moody Scandinavian film with artistic lighting. Mine was more low-budget rom-com directed by a sleep-deprived intern starring Eva Torres, star of the viral video One Day In *Hell*!

Embarrassing? Let's just say if shame were a currency, I could've bought the Bellagio. Twice.

I flicked the AC knob. It coughed out air that smelled suspiciously of regret and Dollar Tree sunscreen. Outside, a tour group shuffled past, their sun hats drooping like wilted lettuce. One woman fanned herself with a poker chip.

Felicia's ETA pinged in my head: 7-10 business days.

To pass the time, I counted the cracks in my dashboard. (Twelve. One resembled Harry Styles.)

The steering wheel burned my palms. I sighed. At this rate, my car would double as a sweat lodge. Maybe I could monetize it? Vegas's newest attraction: The Sauna of Shame!

Last week, waiting for Felicia had been almost pleasant. I'd parked a block and a half away from Desert Bloom by the florist's shop, where bougainvillea spilled over the wall like a Pinterest dream. The owner—a woman who looked like she'd been born holding a pair of pruning shears—had side-eyed my car at first. But once she realized I wasn't casing the joint, just loitering for 20 minutes max, she'd warmed up. She even waved once, which I took as permission to keep freeloading on her floral ambiance.

Note to self: Buy a bouquet. Or at least a single carnation.

Today, though? The bougainvillea looked as wilted as my will to live. I cracked the window, hoping for a whiff of floral serenity, but all I got was a face full of Sahara-grade heat.

Nine minutes down. One to ten to go.

Just as I was about to reset my mental timer, I spotted her. She was power-walking like a woman on a mission, clutching two iced drinks like they were the Holy Grail. Her curls bounced with every step, and her apron—a masterpiece of flour smudges and coffee stains—dangled precariously off one shoulder.

"You're alive!" I called as she yanked open the passenger door.

"Barely," she panted, thrusting a drink at me. "I think I just sweated out my soul."

I started the car and the AC kicked in full-force, filling the space with the scent of iced cortado and stale milk.

"Sorry for making you walk," I said, not entirely sorry. The alternative—showing my face at the café—was unthinkable. And with good reason, too.

Felicia flopped into the seat, fanning herself with a

napkin. "So. Eric was at the café today."

My stomach did a backflip. "Today?"

She raised an eyebrow, clearly too dehydrated to mock me for my overeager tone.

"First time I've seen him in weeks," she added, sipping her drink like it held the secrets of the universe.

"Oh, really," I said, aiming for casual and landing somewhere between "awkward" and "full-on panic."

Felicia smirked. "Yep. He asked about you."

Let me set the scene: Eric Mann—UFC fighter, possessor of a jawline so sharp it could probably file taxes— was a staple at the café. And by "staple," I mean every Saturday at 9 a.m., he'd go in, order a cappuccino, and flash a grin that turned my bones to marshmallow. It was hardly my fault.

This, of course, was before my ex–best friend, Tegan—a human Insta post—declared him her "soulmate" via an elaborate web of lies that would've made *Pretty Little Liars* blush. Spoiler: They weren't soulmates. They weren't even *soupmates*.

The last time I saw Eric, I'd channeled Shakespearean levels of drama in a café full of gawking strangers, while a UFC fanatic live-streamed my meltdown. The video, titled

"Caffeine & Chaos: Love Triangle KO!" now has 3 million views and a comment section arguing whether I'm a "girlboss" or "needs therapy." (*Por que no los dos?*)

Weeks later, the theories persist. Am I Eric's secret wife? A scorned Tinder swipe? A CIA agent investigating latte fraud? The truth? Buried deeper than my gym membership card.

"You should come back," Felicia announced, sidling up to me with the sly grin—or the start of a heat stroke. "Reclaim your Saturdays! Pilates, cortados, that little moan you make when the espresso hits…" She paused, dangling the bait. "Maybe I can save you the last raspberry tart. I'll hide it in my underboob. It'll be squished, but you'll get it, promise!"

I groaned. "You're evil." Ever since the viral video, the café'd been swimming in patrons—which meant, "Sorry Eva, the tarts are sold out!"

Felicia rolled her eyes. "Babe, the internet's moved on. They're all obsessed with a squirrel that learned to skateboard."

"But what if Eric's there? What if he—"

"So what!" She nudged me. "Come on. Your cortisol levels need that tart more than I need a weekend in Hawaii."

"I could use a weekend in Hawaii!" Truth was, I missed it. My Saturdays were more than a routine—they were my foundation. Pilates for the body, caffeine for the soul, and people-watching so prime I'd started mentally casting strangers in rom-coms. (That elderly man with the dachshund? Clearly a retired spy.)

I missed it. More than missed it. Craved it like I craved sunlight and cool air and margaritas and laughter. The misunderstanding of the decade had thrown me into a little depression of sorts, even if it was hard to admit. And a little promise of raspberry tart wasn't good enough to drag me out of it.

"Honestly? I think he's over it."

I glanced at Felicia, stopped at a red light. Her eyes were doing that thing where they looked like they'd been Photoshopped too big, and her hands were jittering so much her iced cortado was practically doing a tap dance. Was it the caffeine? The sun? Or just her desperate attempt to avoid another too-sunny walk tomorrow?

Or—and this was the kicker—maybe she genuinely thought I should just bite it and move on. Who didn't make viral mistakes once in a while?

And I would've moved on, too, if the universe hadn't decided to remind me every time I opened my phone. "UFC

Fuckboy & Café Meltdown Girl Strikes!" the headlines screamed. (Okay, fine, it was just Instagram, but still.)

"I called him a disgusting pig," I groaned, gripping the steering wheel like it might teleport me to a parallel universe. "He's not over that. *I'm* not over that."

Felicia tilted her head, squinting like she was trying to recall the exact wording. "I think you just said he disgusts you. Not the pig part."

I blinked. "That's any better?"

"Marginally."

I buried my face in my hands, the embarrassment hitting me like a rogue wave. "It couldn't have been worse."

"It could've," she said, her tone a perfect blend of sympathy and "can we please talk about something else now?"

"Trust me, Fel. He's not over it. The internet's not over it. Even my dry cleaner brought it up last week."

I pulled into my parking spot, the shade doing absolutely nothing to combat the heat. But I wasn't done yet. I flung open the door, braving the sauna-like air to keep the conversation alive.

"Yeah," Felicia said, though I wasn't entirely sure what she was agreeing to. "But today he asked how you were. I think he gets it was all a misunderstanding. He's not going to hold it against you forever."

My heart did this weird thing where it stopped, then started again like it was on a defibrillator. "He really asked about me?"

A rush of blood flooded my cheeks—part embarrassment, part something else I couldn't quite name. Maybe Felicia was right. Maybe enough time had passed. Maybe we could be friendly again. And maybe, I'd feel brave enough to pick her up at the café instead of lurking by the florist like a creepy stalker.

Felicia flashed a grin, her iced coffee sweating almost as much as we were. "He did. I told him you're still mortified—but thawing, just taking your sweet time. And please thaw, Eva. My blisters have blisters from walking to the damn florist. It's a block and a half! And with this heat, too." She wiggled her foot for dramatic effect.

My gut still knotted at the thought, but a tiny, reckless voice chirped, *If Eric can slide into the café like he's on* Love Island, *why can't you?* Then again, Eric's idea of "confrontation" involved octagons and spandex. Mine involved hiding behind potted ferns.

"I'll Venmo you an Uber," I bargained, fanning myself with too-warm air. "I'm just not ready to be Café Meltdown

Girl: The Sequel."

"Girl, bye," Felicia snapped, her patience evaporating faster than her cortado condensation. "This isn't about the ride. Why can't you get that?"

"But—"

"I'm not finished," she interrupted, her voice rising like a kettle about to whistle. "I'm at the café every day. Eric's back. Even the guy who tried to pay with Monopoly money is back. Why can't you stop hiding?"

I slumped deeper into the driver's seat, now approximately the temperature of a baked Alaska. "I'm not hiding. I'm strategically avoiding."

"Call it what you want." She flopped back, her curls sticking to the headrest. "But someday you'll wake up, 90 years old, yelling at cats about a TikTok literally no one else remembers. Live, Eva. Or Tegan wins."

"Tegan's a sociopath. She'd wear a scandal like it's Zara's new collection."

"Be like me, then!" Felicia gestured wildly, nearly elbowing her door. "I'm out here, unbothered, going to the café day in, day out. People recognize me, but *so what*? It's literally not that hard."

"Fine," I huffed, defeated. "Tomorrow'll be a café

pickup, no more block and a half walk to the florist. But if someone mentions the video, I'm blaming you."

"Deal." She smirked, tapping her phone. "Besides, Eric's still trending on Twitter—I mean, X. Silver linings, yeah?"

I gaped. "His career's one meme away from collapse."

"*Pfft.* UFC's all about drama. He's probably thriving." She flung open the car door, desert heat rushing in like an uninvited in-law. "Now, can we please get out of this mobile sauna before I melt into a puddle of iced coffee?"

CHAPTER

TWO

"EVE-IEEEE," LEXI SINGSONGED BEHIND me, elongating my name like a bad pop chorus.

"You know I'd rather swallow a stapler than answer to that," I snapped, rearranging the gauze pads she'd just upended. Lexi thrived on chaos, especially when it involved "reorganizing" my meticulously stocked drawers into something resembling a Jackson Pollock painting.

"Oh, come on," she grinned, perching on the counter like she owned it—which, given her knack for drama, she practically did. "Angry Eva is my favorite Eva. You're like a disgruntled garden gnome. Adorable."

Lexi was the human equivalent of a chaos gremlin: loud, sparkly, and impossible to ignore. We'd bonded years ago over lukewarm coffee and wild stories about her penchant for gold-digging. My life, by comparison, had all the drama of a

PBS documentary—until now.

"So," she drawled, swinging her legs like a mischievous toddler, "have you checked the view count today?"

Ah. There it was. The reason for her suspiciously sunny mood.

The video. *The* video. The one where I'd accidentally become the internet's favorite "Unhinged Café Girl" and Eric an undeserved "UFC Fuckboy" after my meltdown went viral. Lexi, of course, treated the whole thing like her personal red carpet moment.

"Zero. *Zilch.* I've entered the Witness Protection Program," I lied, restocking tongue depressors with aggressive precision.

"Liar," she sang. "It's at 2.3 million. You're famous, babe! Dr. Patel's niece asked for your autograph yesterday."

I groaned. The only thing worse than being meme-fied was being meme-fied in athleisure. "Lexi, I mentioned your name *once*. You weren't even in the frame, so drop it already!"

"Never!" She waved a hand, nearly knocking over the stethoscope. "I'm basically an influencer now. *Lexi from the Video* has a ring to it, don't you think? Or Influencer Lexi. Lexi with the brand deals?" She kept going.

I stared at her. "You're delusional."

"And you're trending! Own it! Start an OnlyFans for rage therapy!"

"You do it! I'd rather gargle hand sanitizer."

She hopped down, fluffing her hair in the reflection of a sterilized tray. "Relax. In a week, you'll be old news. The internet's already moved on to a cat who can play "Despacito" on a kazoo."

"A cat?"

"With tiny sunglasses. You're basically forgotten, a déjà vu moment."

I chucked a cotton ball at her. "Comforting."

"Always." She winked. "Now, smile for your fans! Mrs. Miller in Exam 3 thinks you're 'spicy.'"

I buried my face in a box of latex gloves. *Spicy*.

God, I missed being PBS.

Lexi, bless her, had turned the social media hurricane into her personal runway. While I'd been busy hiding under bedsheets, she'd posted eleven explainer videos—each windier than the last, complete with a tearful finale that somehow involved her more and more each time. Now, when people Googled "UFC Café Meltdown," they got Lexi's face bathed in Valencia-filtered sincerity. I owed her my sanity, or at least a very large margarita.

"Four million views by lunch!" she announced, trailing me into the stockroom. "By dinnertime, we'll hit five. I've DMd it to everyone."

I restocked Band-Aids to avoid throwing them. "Or—*wild idea*—we could let it die? Like a normal, non-embarrassing human might do with something extremely embarrassing happens to her?"

"Thirty million, Eva. Thirty. Million. That's the goal." Lexi's eyes glazed over, as if envisioning her future villa in Hawaii. "That's influencer territory. Ad deals. Guest judge on that one podcast, the whole bit."

Ah, yes. Lexi's Five-Year Plan: 1) Marry a TFMAM (Trust Fund Middle-Aged Man™). 2) Secure a cameo on *Love Island*. 3) "Accidentally" leak a skincare line à la Hailey Bieber. 4) Be rich enough to finally stop caring?

"It was a *misunderstanding*," I groaned. "If Tegan hadn't —"

"Enough about Tegan!" Lexi fake-swooned against a shelf of antiseptic wipes. "Babe, you're stuck on loop. You gotta let it go. You'll age worse than milk at this rate."

I glared, shoving a box of Band-Aids into a drawer with

unnecessary force. "I have dropped it. It's the whole world who won't drop it—including you."

Lexi paused, her silence thicker than a January detox smoothie. She knew I was still simmering over Tegan like a forgotten kettle, but whereas Lexi saw the viral video as a golden ticket (or at least a discounted path to fame), I saw it as Tegan's personal grenade swaying back into my life.

We'd sworn off "Tegan Talk" weeks ago—after all, why poke a wasp's nest?—but somehow, she always buzzed back in. Probably because Lexi's sugar-daddy, Charles (TFMAM™), and Tegan's fiancé, Scott (a man whose hands resembled dried apricots), were golf buddies who swapped love stories over single malts. Secrets flowed faster than free champagne at their geriatric lunch, and now here we were.

Later, at lunch, Lexi brought the witch back up. "Have you heard the latest on Tegan?"

"I thought you said to forget about T—"

She shushed me with a finger in the air. "This is different. Not your sad little soap opera."

I sighed, giving in. "Fine. What about that liar?"

"I hear there's wedding invites in the air," Lexi hissed, twirling a fork in her pasta. "No prenup, either. Literally none. Charles says Scott's already booked a Maldives villa.

That gremlin won the gold digger lottery in Louboutins."

It hadn't been long ago that Tegan met Scott, her contracted sugar daddy. It had been Lexi who'd introduced the pair. And now, a short few weeks later, Tegan was on her way down the aisle—a gold-plated aisle that would be all her own with the help of one very important little detail: no prenup.

I raised a brow, less surprised than if she'd told me Tegan had taught penguins to tap-dance. "Of course she did. Tegan could fall into a sewer and emerge with a spa voucher."

Lexi's cheek twitched, her usual "I-woke-up-like-this" glamour cracking. "She's set for life, Eva. *Life*. While I'm out here being Charles' plus one for pennies!"

She exaggerated, of course. Charles had been very generous to Lexi, buying her a penthouse, endless luxuries, and a brand new car, a replacement for her (very new) old one. Very generous, indeed. I sipped my too-tart strawberry lemonade and kept my mouth shut. "Relax. Scott's idea of romance is probably gifting her shares in his hedge fund."

"Exactly." She sighed, leaning back on the chair. "Is that too much to ask for?"

"Look on the bright side," Claire said, channeling the optimism of someone who'd just found a crisp $5 in last winter's coat. "Now you can RSVP 'no' and save cash on a waffle iron."

"*No?*" Lexi's gasp could've powered a wind turbine. "I'm going. In head-to-toe vintage Chanel. I'll casually mention my role in her once-in-a-lifetime fortune during cocktails, drop little Easter eggs. By the end, everyone will know it's because of *me* that witch has Scott."

I groaned. "Or you could, you know, *not* feed her ego, let it all go like you tell me to?"

"I'm not all sad and blotchy like you! Bitches rule the world, Eva." She smirked. "Take notes. Or better yet—take revenge. Can't be too emotional to make moves."

"You're being pretty emotional too, Lex. Just in a different way," Claire chimed.

"Let's be real," I said. "Scott's hands felt like a crumpled tax return. She's digging her own grave, anyway."

Lexi snorted, forgetting her man was also a septuagenerian. "An old tax return that can dissolve into nothing at any time. The wedding hasn't happened yet, and she's forgetting that little fact. But now the whole world knows Tegan'd rather snag Eric, but the man wants nothing to do with her. That's the real win. Girl's delusional."

I grinned, though part of me still prickled at the memory. Tegan had spun her web of "Eric and I are totally endgame" lies for months, showing him off like she'd won the relationship lottery. Meanwhile, Eric had been sliding into *my* DMs with the subtlety of a golden retriever in a tennis ball factory. And he'd been in his single-man-looking-for-woman right, too.

If only I'd known.

"Do you think she actually loves him?" Claire mused, nibbling a breadstick twice-dipped in Alfredo. "Or is she just financially committed?"

"Oh, please. She'd marry a sentient piggy bank if it had a trust fund," I said. "But let's not forget—Eric literally shouted 'I'd rather date a cactus' about her in front of 3 million viewers. That video's immortal. Like Gangnam Style, but with more emotional damage."

Lexi cackled. "True. But hey, at least you got the guy's heart. Temporarily. Before you—you know… publicly imploded."

"Thanks," I deadpanned. "But let's be honest—if Eric wanted revenge, he could've just keyed my car. Hasn't done shit, though."

"You haven't been around," Lexi shrugged. "Maybe he's just waiting for the right moment to drop kick you like one of his UFC buddies."

I groaned, tossing a sugar packet at her. "You're the worst. Not like I need any help getting in my already full head."

Claire sighed, stretching her very pregnant belly. "Don't be mean, Lexi. Eric wouldn't do that. If anything, he'd do it to Tegan just to shut her up."

Tegan, of course, had turned the whole debacle into content gold. She'd posted thirst traps set to the viral video's audio—specifically the bit where Eric declares he'd "never in a million years date her." (His words, not mine.) But Tegan just smirked through the pain like a fair contestant who'd just been pied. But I knew her well enough to spot the cracks. Every caption ("Living rent-free!") felt less like a flex and more like a scream into an Hermès handbag (curtesy of Scott).

"Anyway," Lexi said, snapping me back to reality, "Just wanted to vent. Praying Tegan spontaneously combusts at her wedding—if it ever happens! Let us not forget she broke the cardinal rule (i.e.: rule 3) don't sleep with a mark… *yet!*) to do some kinky things, but let's be real—she'll probably just end up inheriting the Hamptons house anyway. *Bitch.*" She huffed, clearly on edge about Tegan getting everything handed to her despite going all *Indecent Proposal* while Lexi had been doing everything by the book and hadn't gotten zilch.

Later, I'd swapped my usual florist detour for Desert Bloom Café—a baby step Felicia would've awarded a gold star. To my shock, the world hadn't ended. No Eric lurking by the succulents. No Tegan photobombing the peonies. Just a close-to-empty parking lot, and not a Tesla in sight. (Bless.)

Felicia slid into the passenger seat, clutching two iced cortados—mine still frosty, a miracle in this heat. "Progress?" she said, happy to have saved the walk.

"Barely. But at least I made it."

"And this," she said, brandishing a nice cortado, "is your reward."

"Hey," I said, a sudden desire lighting me up. "Want to grab a nice bouquet for the house?"

"Only if it's obnoxiously pink."

So we did. And that's how I learned two things: 1) The café's windows didn't shatter when I parked nearby. 2) Hydrangeas fix *everything*.

CHAPTER

THREE

BE GENTLE WITH MY baby," Lexi trilled, blowing a kiss to the valet as her brand-new Porsche glided away like a silver bullet. She clutched her chest dramatically. "I'm in love, Eva. Actual, physical love."

To be fair, Lexi *had* worked hard for that car. If by "hard" you meant strategically deploying her charm in ways that would make a Dubai escort blush. Not that I judged! (Okay, I judged a little.) But Lexi herself had announced over tequila shots, that Charles—her TFMAM (Trust Fund Middle-Aged Man™)—had only earned her back post-Tegan-gate by "investing" in their "future" (i.e.: Porsche Panamera).

"Charles *begged* me to come back," she'd confessed last week, during girls' night. "So I said, 'Darling, if you want my love, buy me a Porsche. Consider it emotional infrastructure.'" She'd winked, as if "emotional infrastructure" didn't sound like a euphemism coined in a Gwyneth Paltrow newsletter. "Men need skin in the game, babe," she'd lectured, as if quoting from *Gold Digger Weekly*. "No feelings without financing!"

The girls and I had theories, of course. Scandalous theories. Had she promised Charles a weekend in a Venetian gondola (at the Venetian, of course)? A themed photoshoot for Easter? A *taxidermy* photoshoot? Lexi's coy smile only fueled the gossip. "A lady never kisses and tells," she'd purred, which was rich, considering she'd been very open about Tegan's bedroom antics. But to be fair, Tegan was no lady.

I gagged a little. "It does drive smoothly," I offered, ignoring the way my own car—a seven-year-old painted a neon green with a faulty heater—coughed like a chain-smoker every time I braked. At least mine came with zero secrets and a clear conscience. Well, mostly clear. If you ignored the time I slathered on SPF on a slimy tourist at the Palms pool for the down payment. Another life.

It was Saturday morning, and I'd already survived Pilates (my ass hadn't). I'd skipped my usual café stop, though— partly to avoid Eric's inevitable "Oh hey, didn't see you there" smirk, but mostly because they'd be out of raspberry tarts anyway. Three weeks straight and counting. At this point, I suspected a conspiracy. A tart-based vendetta. Or just a flock of post-viral video chasers. *Sigh.*

When Lexi texted "Emergency shopping intervention. Wynn. Now." I nearly wept with joy. Not because I craved a $1,000 handbag (who am I kidding, more like a wallet), but because it meant skipping the café *and* dodging Eric one more weekend.

"Did I tell you what Charles made me do for the Porsche?" Lexi purred, linking arms as we glided into the Wynn like we owned it—or at least, like Charles' credit line did. In her four-inch Louboutins, she loomed over me like a glamorous giraffe, while my dupe Lululemon leggings squeaked with every step.

"Let me guess," I said, eyeing a chandelier that probably cost more than my student loans. "Tegan's erotic asphyxiation first date still holds the crown?"

Lexi snorted so hard her Cartier sunglasses slipped. "Please. All I had to do was nibble Charles' toes in the Jacuzzi. Turns out, trust fund babies are weirdly into that. Bastard got his money's worth."

I almost tripped on my own foot. "You what—?"

"Relax! It was nothing." She waved a manicured hand. "He cried. Called me his 'little lobster.' Anyway—" She veered us toward Chanel, her stride radiating the confidence of someone who'd never once had a card decline.

There's a certain magic to trailing Lexi into a boutique. Maybe it's the way sales associates materialize like *Charlie's Angels* extras, fighting to serve her. Maybe it's the scent of debt-free decisions. Or maybe it's Lexi's ability to make "I'll take three Birkins and a lifetime of regret" sound like a brunch order.

"I thought he was an old fart?" I whispered, recalling Charles' liver-spotted hands.

"Only when I'm mad at him." She tossed a tweed jacket at me. "Try this. You look like you've been dressed by a sad PE teacher."

I grimaced at the price tag. "This costs more than my car."

"Your car's a cheapie, Eva. This is an investment." She winked, mouthing "Thanks, Charles" and I knew it would be a little gift from her to me. "Besides, Tegan's probably got a monogrammed yacht now. We're playing catch-up."

I let myself imagine it: Me, gliding into the café, Chanel-clad, Eric spilling his latte in awe. Then I remembered I'd probably trip and stain it with raspberry sauce.

"One day," Lexi said, reading my mind, "you'll stop flinching at price tags and start flinching at cheapies with four wheels."

Lexi's confidence wasn't some bargain-bin impulse buy. Oh no, hers was handcrafted, forged in the fire of a childhood spent learning to weaponize a wink and a smile. While other kids memorized times tables, Lexi perfected the art of batting her lashes at teachers for deadline extensions. ("Life's a buffet, Eva. Grab seconds.") Naturally, she'd long since stopped caring what anyone called her—"gold-digger," "escort," "that girl who dates mummies"—but she drew the line at "ex-stripper." *Nurse*, thank you.

Vegas wasn't kind to women with taste for Rolexes and zero patience for men who went halfsies. But Lexi thrived anyway. Every side-eye from pearl-clutching socialites only fueled her resolve. "Let them gawk," she'd say, fluffing hair extensions. "Jealousy is just flattery in a different font."

Still, she'd broken up with Charles because Scott proposed no-prenup to Tegan before Lexi even got so much as a promise. Work ethic, Lexi'd called it. ("Give an inch, they'll take a mile!")

"Scott folded for Tegan," she declared, striding the boutique like she owned it (or at least rented it hourly). "Charles will crack. Men are like dominos. One falls, the next one follows."

The boutique was the kind of place where the air smelled

like competition and credit card debt. Minimalist racks held three garments total, artfully arranged beside a single crystal vase. My well-loved Nikes squeaked rebelliously on the marble floor, while Lexi—resplendent as always—pored over dresses like a scientist decoding the meaning of life.

I'd just begun mentally pricing the fire extinguisher (5K? 10K?) when a voice sliced through the silence.

"God, Eva, I used to think you dressed like a student on laundry day. Now I see it's a *lifestyle.*"

Tegan. It's like the universe hated me.

There she stood, glowing like a TikTok filter made flesh. Her lips were plumped to Kardashian proportions, her posture so unnaturally erect I suspected a hidden coat hanger. Scott's millions had polished her into something straight off a *Harper's Bazaar* cover—if the headline read "Gold Digging for Dummies."

"Surprised you're not hiding under a rock," I shot back, channeling the bravado of someone who hadn't been reduced to avoiding the café. "Then again, rocks don't have Wi-Fi for your thirst traps."

Her Botoxed brow twitched. *A hit! A palpable hit!*

"Still bitter about Eric?" She fake-pouted. "Funny how you thought he'd ever pick you over me."

"He literally did," I hissed, reminding her of the very public admission. *Eric wanted me!*

"Please," she dismissed me. "He was just angry."

I fake frowned. "Erotomania, isn't it? I looked it up and your face pops up."

"Says the woman who *literally* stalked him into a viral video."

"You'd know all about that wouldn't you? A natural occurring conversation has never crossed your path."

Lexi materialized then, a velvet-clad avenger clutching a dress that screamed "I play in a yacht." "Tegan! How sweet of you to visit. Run along and fetch me a French 75, would you? Extra gin. And do try not to spill it this time—we know how clumsy you get after three martinis."

Tegan's smile froze, her filler-stiff lips quivering like Jell-O in a tremor. "I don't work here."

"Oh?" Lexi blinked innocently. "With that outfit? Fascinating."

I bit back a grin. Leave it to Lexi to weaponize a comeback like it was a designer handbag—sharp, shiny, and devastating. Without her, Tegan would still be hustling champagne in the VIP section, her career trajectory peaking at "eternally tipsy aunt at a bridal shower."

"You're one to talk. Charles won't—"

"Darling," Lexi purred, examining her nails like they held the secrets of the universe, "wasn't Scott your client back when you were slinging cosmos in stilettos? I heard he whisked you upstairs for a… *private tasting*. Must've been a thrilling chase—all five seconds of it." She fake-pouted. "Pity he didn't stick around to teach you CPR."

Tegan's face flickered—pale, then pink, then back to Botox-beige. But shame? Please. Tegan's moral compass pointed squarely toward Sale: 70% Off Dignity.

"Haven't you heard," Tegan drawled, flipping her fresh extensions like a shampoo ad gone rogue, "I've upgraded. From the Wynn Villa to the Nobu Villa. But you wouldn't know luxury if it bit your prenup-phobic ass." She smirked, clearly rehearsing that zinger in the mirror all morning.

Lexi snorted. "Charles funds my life *and* my Chanel habit. Scott gives you… what? A keycard and a senior discount?" She leaned in, stage-whispering, "Does he still think 'ASAP' is a type of aspirin?"

The truth was, everyone knew Tegan's "romance" with Scott Van Hoff—a man whose idea of foreplay was "Let's check your credit score"—was less *Titanic* and more *Pretty Woman*. Sure, she'd landed a lifeboat of cash, but the icing was in the contract.

"I could buy this entire store," Tegan snapped, waving a credit card like a maniac.

Lexi didn't blink. "And I could name-drop the chef at Nobu, but unlike you, I don't confuse money with personality." She air-kissed Tegan's cheek. "Ta-ta, sweetie. I've got a date with a truffle soufflé and a man who doesn't need CPR."

I was halfway to the door, when Tegan threw her grenade, "Tell Eric I forgive him. Must've been so hard for him to trash-talk me like that."

I froze. *Hard?* Eric's rant about her had been an honest rendition of Feelings: The Musical.

"Funny," I said, spinning back with a smile sharp enough to slice butter. "Eric's got a sixth sense for snakes. Took me years to spot the one in my BFF necklace."

Tegan's laugh tinkled like counterfeit coins. "He wants me, Eva. Denial's just his love language."

"The only thing I want," I said, channeling my inner Lexi, "is a lifetime supply of brain bleach to forget your existence. You're a Photoshop job with a credit card. Nothing about you is real. You're practically all air."

Her smirk widened. "I existed when I stole your boyfriend. I existed when Eric was between my legs. Ask him about the night of the red lace. Oh wait—he didn't tell you?"

My lungs staged a mutiny. *Red lace?* I pictured it instantly —*ugh*—alongside Eric's "I'd never be with her!"

"Everyone wants me," she trilled, adjusting her diamond choker like it was a participation trophy.

"Not Eric," I lied, clinging to his version. "He's allergic to Botox and bullshit."

"Oh, please." She waved her left hand, her engagement rock doubling as a weapon. "Scott's ten times the man Eric is. But hey, thanks for the viral clout! My followers doubled, and now Scott's buying me a yacht. You're basically my unpaid publicist."

My brain short-circuited. But my mouth? My mouth was a rogue agent. "Don't thank me," I chirped. "Thank your *creative* bedroom hobbies. Erotic asphyxiation really seals the deal, huh?"

Her jaw dropped. Finally—silence.

I floated out of the store, half expecting confetti to rain down. Behind me, I heard a choked, "How did you—"

Checkmate, bitch.

CHAPTER

FOUR

IF THERE WAS ONE thing I loved more than a Saturday morning cortado (and trust me, that's saying something), it was girls' night. Not just any girls' night, but the kind where the margaritas were frozen, the gossip was hotter than the Nevada asphalt, and the SPF 50 pooled at our feet like a melted popsicle.

Cali's backyard was our official sweat lodge and frozen bar all in one. By "backyard," I mean a Pinterest-worthy oasis with patio lights, a fire pit repurposed as an ice bucket, and enough citronella candles to stage a *Survivor* finale. Sure, the temperature hovered around "surface of the sun," but Cali insisted on hosting like she was auditioning for HGTV Host of the Year.

"It's not heat," Lexi declared, fanning herself with a coaster shaped like a llama. "It's nature's free sauna. We're basically detoxing."

"If I detox any more, I'll evaporate," I muttered, chugging my margarita-slushy hybrid.

Cali, second trimester pregnant and glowing like a radioactive watermelon, waddled over with a tray of virgin mojitos. "Jason's on Rubi duty! He's teaching her to floss. *Teeth*, not dance moves," she added, catching my horrified glance toward the house.

Jason Lopez—Cali's husband, my brother-in-law, and Green Valley's answer to McDreamy (if McDreamy specialized in root canals)—was a saint. The man had mastered the art of "daddy daycare," freeing Cali to host despite her second-trimester exhaustion. Though "hosting" mostly meant she napped upright in a lawn chair while we debated whether Tegan's new yacht would be a marital asset or a midlife crisis.

"Remember when girls' night meant tequila shots and karaoke?" Felicia sighed, eyeing Cali's mocktail.

"Now it's hydration shots and pelvic floor exercises," Lexi said, snapping a selfie with the fire pit. "Progress, babes."

Cali yawned mid-sentence, a skill she'd perfected since becoming a human incubator. "Sorry… Baby's been practicing her drum solo on my bladder."

We'd tried to convince her to take it easy—her first pregnancy had been rougher than a reality TV breakup—but Cali was stubborn. "I need this!" she'd insisted. "Soon I'll be outnumbered by toddlers. Let me pretend I'm fun!"

So here we were, sweating through our linen dresses, while Jason entertained Rubi with a dental mirror and a puppet show about plaque.

"Another round?" Lexi asked, brandishing a blender.

"Is the sun a star?" Felicia shot back, sliding her glass forward.

"I swear, this blend is life-changing," Cali announced, waving a pitcher of margaritas she couldn't drink. "Low-sugar, organic agave, and edible glitter!"

Lexi gasped, clutching her chest. "Glitter? Cali Lopez, are you trying to make us Instagram influencers? Next you'll be staging a TikTok dance in Rubi's playpen."

"Momfluencer is my backup career," Cali deadpanned, adjusting her maternity summer dress with one hand and rescuing a cheese platter from Rubi's grabby fingers with the other. "Jason! Honey! Can you confiscate the cheddar before someone loses an eye?"

Jason emerged, baby monitor clipped to his belt like a SWAT team radio. "On it. Rubi, drop the cheese. *We've talked about this.*"

Cali sighed. "Some days I miss paralegal work. At least subpoenas don't throw tantrums over nap time."

"But subpoenas don't give you this," Felicia said, holding up the glitter tequila bottle like it was the Holy Grail. "This is pure magic. It's like unicorn tears and bad decisions had a baby."

"Speaking of babies," Lexi stage-whispered, "did Eva tell you about her spicy showdown with Tegan?"

Cali's eyes widened. "No, but I've got popcorn. *Jason*! Popcorn!"

As Jason dutifully microwave-popped (parenting MVP), I recounted the mortifying tale. Cali winced. "Eva, you called her a slimy gold digger? To her face?"

"She started it!" I protested. "She implied Eric's come-on was meant for her."

Lexi snorted. "For her? He's publicly denied her."

Felicia raised her glitter shot. "To Eva! Who's out here doing the Lord's work—exposing Tegan's obvious lies."

We clinked glasses. Cali sipped her mocktail, grinning. "Mom life's wild, but this? This is better than cable."

I'd kept Tegan's nuclear-grade bombshell about Eric to

myself, mainly because replaying it in my head made my stomach mimic a rollercoaster designed by a sadist. Felicia knew, of course—Felicia knew everything—but even her promise to "casually interrogate Eric mid-cappuccino" couldn't unknot the guilt coiled in my chest. So what if Tegan and Eric had a history? So what if "red lace" was now seared into my brain like a bad tattoo? Eric and I were… nothing. A blip. A cautionary tale told over rosé.

But Lexi? Lexi smelled drama like a truffle pig in a Gucci trench.

"So there we were," she announced, swirling her margarita like it held the secrets of the universe, "innocently shopping for a dress to stun my trust-fund baby—*details to come*—when who slithers into Chanel? Tegan."

The girls leaned in, their faces lit by the glow of schadenfreude and citronella candles. Even Cali, halfway to a mom coma, perked up. "She's actually engaged to the prune-juice prince? No prenup?"

"None," Lexi said, her voice dripping with envy. "And let's just say her negotiation tactics make my Porsche-forgiveness deal look like a church bake sale." She flicked her wrist, her new Van Cleef bracelet glinting in the sunlight. "But Charles…" She paused, savoring the suspense. "…is considering a prenup edit. And by 'considering,' I mean he bought me this vintage beauty to shut me up while he thinks about it."

Felicia gasped, grabbing Lexi's arm. "Is this the Alhambra collection? The Instagram bracelet? I'm dead!"

"Instagram? Baby, this is real-deal vintage!" Lexi corrected, smirking. "But yes, it's a start. Next step, a tiara. Or a private island. Depends on his stock portfolio."

Cali snorted, rubbing her belly like it was a crystal ball. "No wonder Tegan's out here wife-ing a man who thinks erotic asphyxiation is a form of CPR."

"Oh, she's got him wrapped up like a trick and prioritizing his needs," Lexi purred. "Prioritizing Scott's bank account into her clutch, that is. But let's be real—without her *special skills*, she'd still be hustling bottle service in pleather."

"What kind of special skills?" Claire demanded, leaning forward so aggressively her watermelon-sized baby bump nearly toppled the guacamole. Third-trimester Claire was a force of nature—less "glowing mom-to-be," more "Nancy Drew on a Red Bull bender."

Lexi paused, swirling her margarita with the gravitas of a philosopher pondering the universe. "Let's just say Tegan's upgraded from erotic asphyxiation to *advanced* gameplay."

"The hell does that mean?" Claire barked, hormonal fury

blazing in her eyes. "Spill, or I'll fake labor right here!"

Lexi sighed, like a martyr sacrificing herself for the greater gossip. "Fine. But if your water breaks, I'm not driving you to the hospital." She lowered her voice to a whisper usually reserved for papal secrets. "According to Charles, Tegan and Scott are into *group projects*. And not the PTA kind."

Claire blinked. "A threesome? That's your big reveal? My dog walker's had a threesome."

Felicia nodded sagely. "Threesomes are basically brunch now. Even my grandma dropped hints about her 'wild years' at Easter."

Lexi's eye twitched. "No, you plebs. Not just any threesome. We're talking… accessories. Like, *strap-on* accessories."

The backyard fell silent. Even the cicadas stopped buzzing, as if nature itself needed a moment.

Claire's jaw dropped. "You mean… a… *fake penis* situation?"

"Allegedly," Lexi hissed, clutching her Van Cleef bracelet like a talisman against the visual. "Charles heard it from Scott then ran to tell me all about it."

Felicia choked on her glitter vodka. "With that kind of

service, who needs Netflix?"

Cali, who'd been dozing upright like a narcoleptic flamingo, suddenly snapped awake. "Wait—are we still talking about Tegan?"

"Yup," I muttered, scrolling through Tegan's Instagram. "Girl's lived many lives."

"Hold on—*both* at once?" Felicia gasped, her glitter margarita sloshing precariously close to the rim of her glass. "I thought you meant Tegan hired out for their third wheel. Not hardware." She fanned herself with a napkin. "No wonder there's no prenup. Girl's out here rewriting *Fifty Shades* as a DIY manual."

Cali, suddenly sat bolt upright. "Wait. So Scott wears the strap-on? Or Tegan does? And *why*? Is this a golf metaphor? I don't—"

The rest of us dissolved into giggles, partly from the tequila, partly from the mental image of Scott Van Hoff participating in anything requiring flexibility.

"No, sweetie," Lexi clarified, patting Cali's hand like a patient kindergarten teacher. "Tegan's the one with the strap-on. Scott's just receiving." She paused, then added, "Think of it as reverse golfing."

The backyard erupted into a mix of snorts, gasps, and

Claire accidentally inhaling a tortilla chip. "Why?!" she wheezed, eyes watering. "The visual!"

Lexi sipped her margarita, laughter making the drink wobble. "Babe, Tegan's playing chess while we're out here playing Candy Land. Give a man a lifetime supply of novelty socks, and he'll get bored. Give him novelty *nights*…" She wiggled her Van Cleef bracelet meaningfully. "But mark my words—she's over-leveraging. Men need mystery. Investment. Charles buys me diamonds because I'm a limited edition. Tegan? She's a pop-up shop. Here today, sued tomorrow."

Felicia nodded sagely. "It's like NFTs. All vibes, no resale value."

Cali frowned, rubbing her belly. "So… love is just… financial planning?"

"I wouldn't say love, per se, but companionship yes," Lexi said, pointing her drink at Cali like a courtroom lawyer. "Those of us who know what we want aren't looking for love. We're looking for generational wealth. Tegan thinks she's won, but she's about to get audited."

The group fell into thoughtful silence—or as thoughtful as one can get while debating marital strategies and strap-ons under LED lights.

"Is she using him for money or is Scott using her for her

youth?" Claire said, thoughtful.

"I'd like to think she's the one using him—for obvious reasons—but the reality is that both are using each other. It's a give and take," Lexi continued. "Scott could be using Tegan as his personal fantasy vending machine—insert kink, receive yacht—then dump her at the altar. Classic rich guy move. And Tegan—" She paused dramatically. "Obviously in it for the luxuries."

Felicia snorted. "So Tegan's just hustling? Using the oldest trick in the book? Groundbreaking."

Lexi's eyes narrowed, her siren gaze sharp enough to slice through Felicia's sarcasm. "There's hustling, and then there's *being hustled*. But I get why you're confused. Your idea of 'leverage' is a free cocktail and a Uber home."

Felicia crossed her arms, unfazed. "At least I'm not charging by the hour."

"No, you just donate," Lexi shot back, smirking at Felicia's annual "Oops, I Did It Again" one-night-stand ritual.

Felicia's cheeks flushed. "Excuse me—!"

"Girls," I cut in, waving my hands like a referee at a kitten fight. "Can we *not* turn Tegan's pegging saga into *your* pegging saga?"

Cali nodded, her pineapple-shaped maternity pillow squeaking in agreement. "Save the drama for the next sex scandal."

Lexi sighed, smoothing her Van Cleef bracelet like it was a stress ball. "Anyway. Charles says Scott's basically using Tegan to see how far she'll go. Thinks Scott brought up the no prenup thing to egg her on."

"Sounds like Scott's the user," Cali muttered, earning a chorus of giggles. "Pretty unethical sugar-daddy of him."

"*Pegging!*" Felicia announced, as if she'd just cracked the Da Vinci code. "That's the word! Prince Harry's into it, apparently."

"It's William, actually," Lexi said. *"Allegedly."*

Claire gasped, clutching her bump. "I'm officially a prude. The wildest thing I've done this trimester is eat sushi once. *Uncooked.*"

"That's actually really bad," Cali said.

"Welcome to the club," Lexi said, raising her glass. "We've got T-shirts. 'Vanilla AF'."

"At least we're not honeymooning in the Red Room of Pain," I added, shuddering at the thought of Scott's "putter" collection.

Lexi nodded solemnly. "Charles swears Scott's gone full

Mad Scientist. Tegan's his Frankenstein. *Frankenkink.*"

I was about to ask if Frankenkink came with a Lab safety manual when my phone buzzed. A notification lit up the screen.

"Oh. My. God." I choked, nearly dropping my phone into the guacamole. "Eric Mann just slid into my DMs!"

The backyard exploded.

Felicia lunged for my phone. "Screenshot it!"

Lexi hissed, "Play it cool!"

Cali yelled, "Jason! Bring popcorn!"

And just like that, Tegan's strap-on saga was old news.

CHAPTER

FIVE

"THAT'S GOTTA BE A fake account," Claire declared, leaning over me like a tipsy penguin, her belly bumping the guacamole bowl perilously close to the edge of the table. "No way Eric Mann's sliding into DMs after that video. He's probably hiring a crisis manager, not texting ex-almost-girlfriends."

"It's fake," I agreed, nodding so hard my brain rattled. Between Tegan's creative storytelling and my own verbal grenade-launching at Eric, the odds of him messaging me were slimmer than Lexi's patience with men who went halfsies.

Lexi snatched my phone with urgency. "I follow his *real* account. Let me see—profile pic, blue check, bio that says 'UFC fighter, not a terror'… Yep, it's him." She grinned, handing it back like she'd just validated a winning lottery ticket. "Congrats, babe. You've officially broken the internet *and* his heart."

Felicia fist-pumped the air, nearly spilling her glitter margarita. "Told you he's obsessed! He came by the café twice asking if you'd been back. The man fights people for a living and he's out here nursing a bruise from Eva!"

I stared at the message as if it might morph into a snake.

"Or he's just… grateful," Lexi mused, examining her nails. "His follower count's quadrupled. You're his accidental PR genius. Hashtag meet-cute, hashtag drama."

"Hashtag *public humiliation*," I muttered.

"Puh-lease," Lexi scoffed. "All press is good press. My Van Cleef rep DMd me after the video dropped. We're basically Kardashians now."

Felicia rolled her eyes so hard I worried they'd stick. "You're not a Kardashian. You're a… Kardashian-adjacent."

Lexi glared, eerily close to really losing her patience. "Adjacent?! Honey, I'm the Kris Jenner of this group. *I* make the headlines. *You* make the coffee."

"Girls!" Cali interjected, tossing a cheese cube at them. "Focus! Eva's got a UFC hottie in her DMs, and we're debating Felicia's barista skills?"

Claire, ever the pragmatist, squinted at my screen set to

Eric's Instagram. "What if he's just being nice? Like a golden retriever with abs?"

"Golden retrievers don't hit people for a living and fake an entire relationship," I said, flopping back in my chair.

"In all fairness," Lexi countered, "it was Tegan faking the relationship. Hardly the golden retriever's fault. Besides, this whole thing has been good for him, I bet."

I scoffed. "Good for him? He's probably hiding under a rock as we speak." The Internet hounds had come for me, and I wasn't UFC-fighter-with-an-enticing-dick-print-famous.

"Babe, please," Lexi drawled, fluffing her hair like she'd just stepped off the Blow Bar. "I've gained more followers than a yoga influencer's cork mat. At this rate, I'll be trading Charles for a younger billionaire—one who thinks 'prenup' is a type of smoothie." She paused, raising a brow. "Eric's probably drowning in DMs from thirst traps named Brittany-with-a-Y."

I grimaced, picturing Eric's inbox as a digital meat market. Ugh. My stomach did a backflip worthy of Cirque du Soleil. "Who cares about followers?" I muttered, staring at his message like it might bite.

Lexi threw a cheese block at me. "Followers are currency, Eva! Eric's not just a UFC hottie now—he's a brand. Next stop—cologne ads, protein powder sponsorships, and a *very* tasteful OnlyFans."

Felicia snorted. "Tasteful? His last Instagram story was him in his dick print sweats. He knows what he's doing."

"Exactly," Lexi agreed, for once. "It's about engagement. You wouldn't get it."

"Maybe he's sliding in to apologize!" Felicia chirped. "Or send nudes. Check the message!"

Claire, halfway through her third virgin piña colada, perked up. "If it's nudes, screenshot 'em. Marc's idea of spice is socks with sandals. I need material."

"Claire!" Cali hissed, covering Rubi's ears. "The baby can hear you!"

"Relax, Rubi's future therapist will handle it," Claire said, waving a chip. "Now open the DM. I need a dick pic more than I need a foot rub!"

The girls erupted into giggles—the kind that teetered between shock and delight—as Claire doubled down on her quest for Eric's hypothetical dick pic.

"He's asked me to coffee tomorrow," I said, bracing for the chaos.

Felicia lunged across the table to high-five Lexi, who scowled as she fished a crumpled $20 bill from her Gucci clutch. "*Ugh*, fine. But I still think he'd have moved on to some Instagram yogi by now. Guess Eva's his weakness."

"You're betting against me, Lex?" All fake shock, but she just waved me off.

"Not all men are Scott!" Felicia crowed, waving the cash like a victory flag. "Eric's a golden retriever in human form. He probably hired a skywriter to apologize but settled for DMs."

Sober Claire said, "Please. Golden retrievers don't have biceps that could crack walnuts. But sure, let's pretend he's romantic." She sipped her virgin piña colada, then added, "Still, sliding into your DMs post-meltdown? That's either true love or a very savvy PR move."

Lexi rolled her eyes, "What do you know about PR moves?" Though her smirk betrayed her. "All men are only after two things: admiration from other men and pretty girls to show off—men like Scott, coincidently. He likes romantic walks at the beach and to get choked and pegged for pleasure by a pretty girl he can show off at golf."

I spat my drink. "Christ, not the pegging."

Felicia laughed and said, "Not the walk on the beach."

Cali, ever the diplomat, tossed a cheese cube at them. "Focus! Eva's got a date with Vegas's most viral UFC snack. Do *not* wear those sweatpants with the hole in the crotch."

"Hey, those are my emotional-support pants!" I protested, but the table was already spiraling.

"Speaking of," Claire interjected, rubbing her belly, "Tegan's the one choking old men? I thought she was the one getting choked."

"What's that gotta do with pants," Felicia asked, though Claire just shrugged.

"Babe," Lexi drawled, "when your date's on his third Viagra, everyone's getting choked. Tegan's out here playing *Fifty Shades* with Scott's trust fund. No rules, just chaos."

Felicia fake-gagged. "Now I'm picturing Scott in a leather harness. Thanks for that."

"*Classy* leather harnesses, mind," Lexi clarified, wagging her margarita glass. "I'd demand a Cartier collar minimum. Tegan's giving us real gold diggers a bad name—no fincsse! You can't just hand over the goods pre-contract. Amateur hour."

"It worked for her," I said, playing devil's advocate again.

"She got lucky!"

The girls howled, and even I cracked a smile. Lexi's "romantic strategies" sounded like a corporate merger, but her point landed: Tegan's playbook was all risk, no reward. Or perhaps *all reward*? Jury was still out.

"One could argue Tegan's *eagerness* is why she's sprinting down the aisle with a man who thinks a seven day honeymoon to the Maldives is a sale rack at Ross," Claire mused, rubbing her belly like it was a crystal ball. "No stretch marks, no midnight feedings—just infinity pools and room-service tiramisu. Kinda jealous."

Lexi snorted, nearly upending her margarita. "Oh, please. Scott's 'investment' in her is thinner than his hairline. A few Birkins and a Rolex? Please. That's pocket change for a man who summers in places ending with '-iza.' And that's if he marries her—and it's still a big *if*."

"A man needs to invest in a woman to see a value. Something about their brains being wired to dollar sigs or something or other," I said, regurgitating lessons Lexi had given me throughout the years. "Women cost, and they know it."

Cali blinked, her mom-brain visibly buffering. "Wait, *costs*? Like emotional labor? Or… literal costs?"

"Both," Lexi said, slamming her glass down like a gavel. "Women are luxury items, babe. We're the human equivalent of a limited-edition Birkin—rare, high-maintenance, and *never* on sale. Hair? Weekly upkeep. Nails? Art installations. Periods? A blood sacrifice to the uterus gods. Men think we're 'free-to-play,' but honey, we're subscription-only."

Claire gasped, clutching her bump. "Lexi! Rubi's learning vowels." But Rubi was somewhere inside watching Cocomelon.

"Good! Teach her early. *Value thyself.*" Lexi tossed her hair, her Van Cleef bracelet clinking like a cash register.

Cali shook her head, her mom bun bouncing like a disapproving metronome. "Love's not a spreadsheet, Lexi. It's about connection, not cost-per-click."

Lexi's glare could've curdled the margarita mix. "Oh, please. That Pottery Barn-perfect outdoor living set? The pool that sparkles like Felicia's glitter tequila? You don't think Jason's dental drills paid for all that? Honey, you signed a contract the minute you said 'I do.' Mine's just itemized and signed way before."

Cali opened her mouth—then snapped it shut, outmaneuvered by Lexi's ruthless retail logic.

"Exactly," Lexi purred, victory dripping from her Van Cleef bracelet. "You traded vows for a Wolf stove. I trade *attention* for a Porsche. Same game, different checkout lines."

Felicia, ever the chaos gremlin, leaned in. "But if Scott's getting all his kinks comped for free—or close to free— what's stopping him from ghosting Tegan? Dude could vanish faster than my self-respect after tequila."

Lexi paused, savoring the spotlight. "Tegan's a pop-up shop—here for the 'gram, gone by Black Friday. I'm a heritage brand. Charles knows my value is all appreciation, not depreciation. Scott? He's got no skin in the game. Tegan's like a Netflix trial—he'll cancel before the free month ends."

I sipped my drink, picturing Tegan's wedding: Scott grinning like a garden gnome in a tux, Tegan photoshopped into a Stepford wife. "So if he bolts, she's left with what? A closet of Birkins and trust issues? No real skin, right?"

"Please," Felicia snorted. "She'll 'accidentally' get pregnant. Khloé Kardashian 101."

Lexi nearly choked on her olive. "Scott's got more kids than a *Kindergarten Cop* reboot. His child support's capped tighter than my jeans post-COVID. Tegan's not a wife—she's a subscription he'll cancel mid-season."

Claire, wide-eyed, whispered, "Marc wants to try butt stuff. Should I charge him for that or…"

The table froze. Even the ice cubes stopped clinking.

Lexi patted her hand. "Sweetie, if he wants backdoor access, charge him a resort fee. And buy a *really* good lube."

CHAPTER

SIX

⌒

THE BELL ON THE the café door chimed, and the scent of espresso hit me like a hug from a caffeinated angel. Felicia squealed, nearly upending a tray of macarons. "You're here!" she trilled, executing a shimmy and slide behind the counter. "Knew you'd cave. It was Eric's DM? Was it?"

"No," I lied, my cheeks betraying me with a nuclear blush. Sure, Eric's message had pinged my heart like a rogue pinball. But admitting that felt like handing Tegan a loaded meme generator, even if she was out of the picture. PTSD and all that.

Felicia smirked, sliding me a cortado extra ice, and no, it wasn't an americano no matter how much the ice melted. "Nothing wrong with a man who apologizes for *your* outburst, Eva. Just a good man with good intentions, I think."

"It was a misunders—"

"Right, a misunderstanding." She pushed a curl behind her ear, eyes darting to Shane who was in the background trying not to yell at a patron who'd complained about an order. "Go on, I'll bring out your order."

I fled to my corner table, the one with the wobbly leg and a view of the garden graveyard. The newly planted roses had died already, and had been dug up already. RIP. Two pages into my book (How to Stop Sabotaging Your Life in 10 Easy Steps—irony: 10/10), the air turned Arctic.

Tegan.

No fucking way.

She swept in like an unwanted tornado, her lips plumped to oblivion and a Birkin dangling like a trophy. "Eva," she purred, looming over me like a Botoxed vulture. "Still clinging to your sad little routine, I see. Pilates, cortado, and existential dread—how *quaint*."

"What do you want, Tegan? A DNA sample? A kidney?" I'd give her Eric just to be left alone.

"Darling, I have everything." She flashed a diamond the size of a ice cube. "Scott's finally making an honest woman of me. No prenup." She paused, savoring my eye-roll. "Oh, and you're not invited. Unless you'd like to valet park? You've got the face for it."

I sipped my coffee, channeling the zen of a woman who'd survived both a viral scandal and IKEA on a Saturday. "Funny, I heard he's into 'equals.' Guess that explains the prenup panic."

Her smile faltered. "Panic?"

"Mmm. Six lawyers, wasn't it? Or was that your bachelorette guest list?" I hadn't heard diddly squat, except for some very detailed bedroom behavior, but her reaction had been worth it.

Felicia materialized, wielding a raspberry tart like a shield. "Tegan! Love the filler. Is that the 'I'm compensating for a personality' collection?"

Tegan's nostrils flared. "Enjoy your budget latte, Eva. Some of us have weddings to plan." She kept going, talking about wedding this and Scott that.

"Sure," I said, leaning back in my chair with the kind of faux-casual confidence that screamed "I've got receipts and you're not gonna like them." Tegan might've been gliding around in Valentino heels now, but I remembered the days when her idea of a good time was swiping my lame boyfriend and getting me fired from low-level pool duty.

She paused mid-monologue, which was impressive

because she'd been talking to herself for a solid five minutes. Something about being Scott's "equal" and how their love was "a meeting of minds" (i.e.: a meeting of his bank account and her Instagram).

"Tegan," I said, stirring my latte with the calm of someone who'd watched true crime for sport and knew exactly how to legally dispose of a human body, "I don't care. So, please. Leave. Me. Alone."

She laughed—a deep, belly-chortle that probably cost $500 in Botox upkeep. "Darling, alone is your brand. Still mad about my little truth bomb? Red lace, Eric in my bed. Aww." She fake-pouted, her lips resembling two overinflated pool toys.

My fists clenched. "You're a known liar, Tegan. Nothing you say has weight."

She giggled, her eyes lighting up like she'd just won. "Oh, Eva. You're so easy."

I backpedaled. "Not that it matters, but Eric and I are just friends—"

"Truth hurts, I know. Toodle-oo," she sang, sashaying out.

I took a deep breath, resisting the urge to hurl my tart at her retreating figure. Felicia appeared, sliding a fresh raspberry tart onto my table like a peace offering.

"I hate her," she said, glaring at Tegan's retreating form. "She only came to gloat. That woman's soul is made of darkness and spite."

"Worse," I muttered. "She's made of fillers and lies. All lies."

Felicia's eyes widened. "What if she sent you that DM? Pretending to be Eric?"

My breath hitched, but I forced it back down like a rogue hiccup. Tegan was still at the counter, ordering her coffee in those six-inch Valentino heels—the ones with the chunky sole that screamed "I'm rich, but I can still run from my problems." I silently prayed her latte was scalding.

"Lexi said the account was real," I muttered, more to myself than Felicia.

"Well, Mr. Dick Print (Eric's unfortunate nickname still stuck some days) hasn't graced us with his presence all morning," Felicia said, wiping down the table with the precision of a crime scene cleaner. "Wonder what that means."

"I didn't come here for him," I said, letting the sentence dangle. The truth was I'd been low-key hoping Eric would waltz in with his usual charm—maybe a croissant, maybe a sheepish grin. But after my very public crash out, I couldn't blame him for ghosting. Plus, Tegan's little "red lace" revelation was still rattling around my brain like a loose marble.

Fucking Tegan.

"I know, honey," Felicia said, patting my hand like I was a spooked horse. She didn't push, bless her.

Just as Tegan sashayed toward the door, coffee in hand and smugness radiating like cheap perfume, the door swung open. And there he was.

Eric.

He looked like he'd been marinating in sunlight—golden, glowing, and unfairly gorgeous. My stomach did a backflip, which I promptly ignored. He held the door open for Tegan, and I had to physically stop myself from rolling my eyes.

"Eric, darling," Tegan purred, running a hand over his chest like she'd once owned it. "Make sure you RSVP to the wedding. It'll be the event of the decade. You won't want to miss it."

Eric didn't push her away. He just stood there, his expression unreadable, while my brain conjured images of them together that I *really* didn't need. "I'll think about it," he said, almost too soft for me to hear. It made me think of ungodly things. Things like, *maybe she's right and he's lied about everything, I mean, just look at the way he talks to her, it's intimate and*—ugh!

"I know we've had our bad moments," Tegan continued, her voice dripping with faux sweetness. "But let's let bygones be bygones, yeah?" She reached up, caressing his cheek like they were in a soap opera.

Finally, Eric stepped back, his jaw tightening. "Tegan," he said, his tone flat. "Stop that, will you?"

She backed away, but like always, laughed it off. "Think about it."

I held my breath, waiting for the drama to unfold.

"I will," Eric said, letting the café door swing shut with a *whoosh* that felt oddly cinematic. He ambled to the counter, flashing me a sideways glance and a smile so unfairly charming my heart did a salsa number—traitorous organ, that one.

The last time I'd seen him, I was "Unhinged Café Girl," and he was "UFC Fuckboy." Now, here he was, glowing like a human caramel latte, while I sat there in my Lululemon knockoffs, trying not to spill my cortado. Tegan's little performance still clung to me like bad perfume, but Eric's dimples were working overtime to distract me. *Damn him.*

After ordering (a cappuccino, extra cocoa), he slid into the seat across from me like he'd never left.

"Hi," he said, his voice softer than a cashmere throw pillow. His eyes—those stupidly perfect navy-blue eyes—crinkled at the corners, and I felt my emotional fortress develop a suspicious crack. *Too soon, Eva! The jury's still out.*

"Hi," I replied, my smile betraying me entirely. It was easy to forget what a nasty pig's breakfast I'd made of things, wasn't it.

"I'm sorry about that. Tegan's," he started, grimacing like he'd bitten into a lemon.

"Don't," I cut in, sharper than I intended. I didn't need the Tegan 101 recap. "She's a human glitter bomb. Boundaries aren't in her vocabulary."

He chuckled, raking a hand through his hair—a move so practiced it should've been insufferable, but nope. "Accurate. She's... a lot."

I fiddled with my spoon, suddenly hyper-aware of my sweaty palms. *Alexa! Add to cart industrial-strength antiperspirant.* "Eric, I'm—"

"Don't," he interrupted gently, leaning in. "This place? It's you. Quirky, cozy, mismatched mugs and all. Don't let any of this stuff chase you out. For the record, the video wasn't that bad. I've had worse Mondays."

I snorted. "You're just saying that because you looked

fine as hell yelling, 'I'd rather date a cactus!'"

"Did you say *fine*?"

My eyes snapped open. "I meant—"

"Kidding," he said, a sly smile on his lips. "But did I say the cactus thing?" He rubbed his chin.

"Allegedly," I replied, though I'd definitely added some creative flair to the video in my head. He only grinned.

"Seriously—it's water under the bridge. Or, in our case, espresso under the table? Too cringe?"

I laughed, tension dissolving like sugar in my drink. "Tegan's a pain in the neck, but… thanks. For not, you know, ghosting me like a sane person."

His smile faltered, sincerity flooding his gaze. "Eva, the whole thing was a dumpster fire. But I get why you thought what you thought. I should've been clearer. It was all a misunderstanding."

"That's what I've been saying! It was a *misunderstanding*."

He chuckled, "Me too. It's turned into a whole mess, hasn't it."

"A derailed mess," I said.

"Or perhaps a bridge?"

The nervous giggle slipped out before I could stop it—a

sound somewhere between a hiccup and a startled poodle. Eric chuckled, his laugh warm and effortless, like he'd been genetically engineered to disarm awkward women. *Damn him.*

"I was so wrong," I admitted, my voice barely above a whisper. Despite the lingering echo of past drama, a tiny spark of hope flickered in my chest, like a faraway light in a sea of despair.

"No grudges here," he said, leaning in his chair with the kind of ease that made me wonder if he'd ever stressed about anything in his life. "If anything, I respect you more. You handled that mess like a pro—even if you did call me a 'UFC fuckboy.'"

I smiled, despite the nerves igniting me. "I'm pretty sure that was the internet."

"Right. You called me a disgusting pig, then."

My cheeks flamed. "Wrong again. I simply said 'you disgust me.'"

A laugh bubble escaped him, and I allowed myself a tiny lingering look. *Gorgeous.* "Marginally better. All's forgiven."

My face betrayed me with an involuntary smile. *Stupid dimples.* "Thanks. Huge weight off my shoulders, really. But if Lexi's right, you owe me a thank you. Your social media's gone full Kardashian."

He laughed, shaking his head. "Oh, yeah, thanks for the career boost. It's been insane. Doors I've been knocking on for years just swung open. My DMs are now 90% thirst traps, 10% death threats."

"It's all about balance," I said, grinning like a roast pig. "I'm glad something good came out of it."

And there it was again. The look. A look that said "I've been thinking about you and now you're right here, in front of me." *Damn him.* And just as quick, it was gone, replaced by something much less intense.

"Maybe we can do it again when my career falls off, this time you'll call me a 'charming bastard' instead of a 'disgusting pig.'"

"I didn't say 'disgusting pig!'"

"Right!" He said, laughing. "Funny how it replays as 'pig' in my head. Or maybe 'pug,' that's better? 'You disgusting pug, you!'"

I snorted. "No! I didn't say anything of the sort."

"Well, whatever it was, thank you all the same."

I couldn't help my smile. "Lexi says I deserve a cut of your sponsorship deals. Maybe a lifetime supply of protein shakes?"

"Done. But first—" He leaned in, suddenly serious. "I've got a fight in May. Big one—against Joey Carrano, the reigning champ. Ever heard of him?"

I shook my head. "I know diddly squat about UFC."

Eric barked a laugh. "That's perfect! Point is, I want you there. And Felicia, of course. VIP tickets. Free merch. The works."

My heart did the salsa thing again. *Was this a date? A guilt trip? A tax write-off?* "I'll come," I said, "I'll even bet on you. Consider it my apology for accidentally launching your career."

He laughed, deep and rich, like his voice had been aged in a whiskey barrel. "Deal." His fingers brushed mine—a touch so fleeting I might've imagined it. (I didn't.)

There it was again, that look in his eyes. The one that said *in another life, we'd be slow-dancing to Ed Sheeran right now*. But before he could speak, I yanked my hand back like it'd been scalded by a rogue cappuccino steamer.

"Great," he said, clapping his hands together like he'd just closed a business deal. "Saturday. Here. Don't be late," he said, standing to leave.

"Great," I echoed, my brain screaming.

As he walked out, Felicia materialized, eyes wide. "Were you *flirting* with Eric Mann?

I sank into my chair, letting the emotions run through me.

"I have no idea."

CHAPTER

SEVEN

THE CAFÉ HUMMED LIKE a beehive that had just discovered espresso, all signs of a Tegan-induced struggle evaporated into the ether. Saturday morning chaos reigned, toddlers hurling croissants, Shane juggling oat milk cartons, and a man in the corner passionately debating the merits of "cold brew vs. drip" with a hurried Felicia. I slumped at my usual table, nursing a cortado and the emotional hangover from my morning duel with Tegan.

And Eric. Sweet, confusing, dimple-equipped Eric.

Felicia materialized like a glitter bomb in a apron, her eyes sparkling with the intensity of someone who'd mainlined three Red Bulls. "Spill. Now. What did She-Who-Must-Not-Be-Named say? And don't skip the bit where Eric blew her off."

"She's marrying WhatsHisName," I said, waving a spoon like a tiny sword. "Scott. The human ATM with a yacht."

Felicia gasped. "*No*. That's official now? But he's got the charisma of a wet sock, and older than dirt! How?"

"Apparently, 'erotic asphyxiation' is his love language. Who knew?"

"Oh, Tegan." She shuddered.

"I just wish she'd leave us alone. Why come here when she's been publicly denied by Eric? It's not like she has any business here, except to make our life just a little bit nasty, isn't it?"

"I'd ban her, but Guy says she's 'good for business.'" She jerked a thumb at the café owner—Guy. "Though if followers paid the rent, we'd all be living in Tegan's DMs."

"Can we not talk about her? I've hit my daily quota of narcissism."

"Fine." Felicia leaned in, her grin widening. "What about Eric? Don't think I didn't see those heart-eyes emojis you were mentally texting him."

I cringed. "He invited me to his UFC fight. VIP tickets. As friends, of course."

Felicia's jaw dropped. "Friends? Sweetie, men don't give VIP tickets to 'friends.' They give them to women they want to impress before declaring, 'I've secretly loved you since the viral video where you called me a disgusting pig!'"

"He did *not*—"

"—yet!" She hit the table with her palm. "This is a rom-com meet-cute! You'll be ringside, he'll KO some guy named Brick the Dick, and you'll kiss in a haze of confetti and protein powder!"

"It's Joey Car-something. And you're coming."

She squealed. "I am? Oh, this just keeps getting better and better!"

"It's a peace offering, I'm sure. Nothing more. At least it gets rid of the awkwardness."

"But he touched your hand! Electrifyingly, you said! That's not 'just friends'—that's *Hallmark Movie* territory if I've ever seen one."

"It was a micro-touch, Fel. Barely registered it." I sipped my latte, ignoring the way my traitorous pulse did a salsa three-step at the memory.

Felicia drummed her nails on the table, a gleam in her eye. "You should've asked him point-blank: Did you or did you not Netflix-and-chill with Tegan? He'd have cracked! Men always do under direct sunlight and scrutiny."

"Ah yes, because nothing says 'Let's be friends' like

ambushing him with 'So, screw any sociopaths lately?'"

She sighed dreamily. "We'll never know now. Though if he did, maybe Tegan taught him that thing she does with Sc
—"

"*No*." I slammed my cup down, splashing cortado. "We are *not* dissecting Tegan's wild sex agenda. Or Scott's. Or anyone's."

"Fine," she huffed, then perked up. "But what if the tickets are fake? What if it's all a ruse to strand you in a parking lot with a 'Gotcha!' banner?"

I grinned, tossing a sugar packet at her. "Then I'll live-stream it and go viral. Again. 'Unhinged Café Girl: Redemption Arc.' Hashtag *blessed*."

Felicia cackled, dodging the sugar packet. "Just promise me one thing. If he does declare undying love mid-fight, you'll yell 'KO me, Daddy!' for the 'gram."

"Shut up, Felicia," I laughed, throwing another sugar packet. At this point, my dignity was already six feet under. What's one more shovel?

"Oh, for the love of—!" Lexi yelped, barreling past me in the hallway of Boring Nondescript Medical. I'd been mid-stride, clutching a patient file titled "Mr. Levi's Mysterious Rash", when she hip-checked me into a potted fern. The fern, I noted grimly, handled the collision better than I did.

"What in the actual hell is happening?!" I hissed, untangling myself from foliage.

"Claire's water broke!" Lexi shouted over her shoulder, already halfway to the supply closet.

I froze. Claire? *Our* Claire? The one whose baby wasn't due until *after* her meticulously planned "Fetal Beyoncé" themed shower next week? My brain short-circuited, imagining a tiny newborn in a glittery leotard. "But… she's only 34 weeks!" I squeaked.

Lexi reappeared, arms stacked with towels like she'd just robbed a hotel linen cart. "Yes, and the baby missed the memo!" She bulldozed past, leaving me gawking at the scene. Claire, our normally unflappable receptionist, was now sobbing into her "World's Best Mom" mug (a gift from her future child, ironically), while amniotic fluid pooled artistically around her desk chair.

"Eva!" Lexi barked, snapping her fingers in my face. "Stop fainting at the sight of amniotic fluid and *call 911*!"

"Right! Yes! Life-saving! On it!" I fumbled for my phone,

accidentally opening a 4-day-old Uber Eats order for pad Thai instead. Lexi, meanwhile, had transformed into an ER-sanctioned superhero—calmly coaching Claire through breaths while fashioning a makeshift diaper out of sterilized gauze. I'd seen her handle entitled trust fund babies at the club, but *this*? This was her magnum opus.

"Claire, honey, where's your phone?" I asked, after finally dialing the ambulance. "Need to call your husband."

"He's at the golf course," she wailed, as if he'd announced he was joining Cirque du Soleil. "He doesn't even answer when I send meme texts!"

The paramedics arrived, looking unfairly handsome for people tasked with hauling a sobbing woman through a lobby decorated with "Trust me, I'm a Doctor!" posters. Lexi shoved me toward the ambulance. "Go with her. I'll meet you there once I've dealt with everything here."

Three hours, two wrong turns, and one paramedic named Greg (who I'm 80% sure winked at me) later, it hit me. *Felicia.*

"Shit," I gasped, clutching my phone like a lifeline. "I'm supposed to pick her up in ten!"

She answered first ring. "Felicia, you'll never believe what happened," I blurted, launching into the saga of Claire's Preemie Panic while pacing the hospital linoleum like a caffeinated flamingo. "She's in delivery, Marc's probably still clutching a golf club for moral support, and the baby's out here auditioning for 'World's Most Dramatic Entrance.'"

Felicia gasped. "Is the baby okay? *Is Claire okay?* Should I burn sage? Call a priest? Bake a casserole?"

"All of the above," I said, sagging into a chair that smelled faintly of antiseptic and regret. "But mostly, just send good vibes. And maybe a beta blocker."

"Go be Claire's hero," Felicia ordered. "I'll hitch a ride with someone, maybe get an Uber."

By the time Marc stumbled into the waiting room—hair wild, eyes wider than Lexi's Amex limit—Lexi and I had stress-eaten three vending machine Twixes and debated baby names ("Beyoncé Jr." vs. "Fern"). Marc flopped beside us, clutching his phone set to a photo of a tiny, wrinkly human who resembled a disgruntled garden gnome. "Meet Baby," he croaked. "He's perfect. Also, why does he look like he pays taxes?"

Lexi cooed, "A future hedge fund manager! Look at those cheekbones," while I teared up at Claire's text: "Alive. Send sushi."

Later, when Lexi was driving me home, she offhandedly said, "Claire's a mom. I hardly believe it."She swerved around a pothole like an F1 driver. "Next she'll be hosting

Peppa Pig marathons and arguing about stroller brands on Babycenter."

"She'll crush it," I said. "Remember when she negotiated a 50% discount on hemorrhoid cream? Born to parent."

Lexi's grip tightened on the wheel. "Eva what if *I* want a baby?"

I choked on the last bit of Twix. "You? The woman who calls strollers 'stroll-zombies'? Who said infants smell like 'regret and milk vomit'?"

"Not just *any* baby," she clarified, eyes gleaming. "A trust fund *baby* baby. Picture it, tiny Gucci booties, a nursery designed by Gwyneth Paltrow, and an au pair named Manon."

"Ah, so Charles just needs to live long enough to fund a *Goop* nanny suite," I teased. "Better start feeding him kale smoothies."

"Eva!" She swatted me, nearly sideswiping a cyclist. "Charles is a bull. He'll outlive us all, if only to spite the taxman."

Once home, I barely toed off my shoes before Felicia pounced, eyes blazing with the fervor of a woman who'd mainlined gossip straight from the tabloids. "Bitch, guess what? You're gonna die!"

My brain, already fried from the day's chaos, immediately conjured images of alien abductions or Felicia adopting a feral raccoon.

"What?" I squeaked, clutching the doorframe like it might save me from whatever fresh hell awaited. "Did you crash my car? Burn down the café? *What?*"

Felicia rolled her eyes, excitement bubbling. "Relax, drama queen. Nothing actually worth dying for."

"Felicia, please. After the day I've had," I protested, kicking off my Crocs. "Lexi hip-checked me into a fern today. Claire went into unexpected labor, and I'm beat."

She game me a sharp look. "Claire's the one who birthed a human today, not you. Though, honestly, your cortisol levels could power the Strip."

I returned it.

"Anyway," she plowed on, ignoring my trauma, "guess who played Knight in Shiny BMW when my Uber canceled?"

"Shane?" I guessed, naming the café's resident latte artist/resident patron fighter.

"Nope."

"The guy who stares at you like you're a walking caramel macchiato?"

"He does not stare—"

"He lingers," I countered, miming exaggerated heart eyes. "Like a golden retriever outside a butcher's shop."

"It. Wasn't. Him." She paused, grinning like she'd just won the lottery and planned to spend it all on Tegan's tears.

"Oh, for Pete's sake, just tell me!"

"It was Eric! Eric Mann. UFC Fuckboy, cappuccino lover, your future baby daddy—"

The room did a full *Inception* spin. "Eric drove you here? In a car?"

"No, we flew, actually."

"Oh my fucking god."

"Shocking, right?" Felicia flopped onto the couch, a smug smile on her face. "Turns out he's got a BMW. It must be new because I've never seen it. Had you? Also—" She leaned in, lowering her voice like we were plotting a heist. "—he asked about you. *Twice.*"

My jealousy/curiosity/excitement did a backflip, tangled with panic, and face-planted into confusion. "What kind of asking?"

"The casual kind. 'How's Eva post-scandal?'" She air-quoted, then dropped the bomb. "And he had a lot to say."

"What did you do, Felicia?"

"Pour us wine. You're gonna need it."

CHAPTER

EIGHT

"TELL ME AGAIN WHAT he said!" I barked, pacing our tiny kitchen like a deranged runway model in fuzzy socks—nearly colliding with the countertop's corner as I flailed about.

Across the table, Felicia slumped, cradling her tea like it was the last vestige of her sanity. "For the fourth time, Eva," she sighed. "He said he liked you. You gave him vibes colder than a Costco freezer, so he backed off. That's it."

"That is *not* it!" I squawked, accidentally sending a jar of wooden spoons tumbling to the floor. "This isn't some rom-com montage, Fel! Did he mention Tegan? Did he call me 'Unhinged Café Girl'? Did he—oh my god—quote that viral video line?"

Felicia let out a long, exasperated sigh, the kind a woman

might make if she'd rather be dissecting Tegan's prenup with a cheese knife. "No, Eva. He was actually really nice. A proper gentleman, really."

I froze mid-step, clutching a spatula like it was my gavel. "Again. Tell me, word for word."

"I've told you already," Felicia mumbled into her mug.

"Word. For. Word." I jabbed the spatula at her, eyes wide. "Did he smirk? Did he hesitate? Did he mention the whole misunderstanding?"

"The misunderstanding?" Felicia blinked slowly. "Eva, that was ages ago."

"Ages ago?" I gasped, as though she'd just uttered Voldemort's name. "That's literally the major incident here! It's crucial!"

"Right. Here we go again," she said, rolling her eyes so hard I nearly heard them clatter. "Look, he overheard you cancelling my ride, then played knight in shining armor, and well—the rest is history."

"Felicia," I warned, half-amused, half-horrified.

"Fine," she relented, "that's when I asked him if he still got night sweats thinking about you."

"Oh my god!" I lunged across the table, sending salt shakers flying in dramatic slow motion. "You didn't—tell me you didn't—"

"Relax!" Felicia interrupted, grinning mischievously. "He laughed! Said it's mostly when you're mean to him."

I screamed into a pillow.

She leaned back in her chair, clearly pleased with herself, as if she'd just dropped the plot twist of the century. "Honestly, Eva, he's way more chill than you give him credit for. Seriously, he's chill—like, way chill—more chill than you, who once cried because a barista misspelled your name as 'Eba.'"

"Come on, who spells it Eba? That barista misspelled my name on purpose."

Felicia sighed, clearly regretting her decision to share anything. "He said he tried getting closer to you every time he saw you, but after finding out he was just a revenge plot gone bad—"

"Because Tegan *lied to me*!" I blurted, nearly knocking over a potted basil plant.

"—he thought you were just being mean. Cut him a break, Eva. It's his right to feel wronged."

"So, what exactly did he say about Tegan?" I demanded, pacing the kitchen like a detective interrogating a suspect. "Why'd she lie about him? And—just to clarify—is she *still* lying?" Hello, red lace. Ugh.

Felicia groaned, slumping into a chair like she'd just run a marathon. "Eva, I've told you this already. Do you need me to write it down? Get it tattooed on your arm?"

"Tell me again," I shot back, giving her my best glare.

She groaned. "Fine. He says he's never dated her. And, honestly, he looked uncomfortable when I brought her up. Apparently, she's been following him around like a groupie, hopping from gym to gym, trying to land a UFC guy."

I blinked. "Tegan? The one who looks like she stepped out of a *Vogue* shoot and smells like Tom Ford's Fucking Fabulous?"

"Yep. That Tegan." Felicia grimaced. "According to Eric, she's already been through half his friends. He's not into sloppy thirds."

A cold shiver ran down my spine. "What if he's lying?"

Felicia snorted. "Eva, does it even matter? Whether he slept with her, whether he didn't, whether he's into you or not—it's too late. He's been through enough drama. I get why he'd want to keep it just friends at this point."

"That's a little harsh, don't you think?" I muttered, but my voice lacked conviction.

She arched a brow.

I collapsed into a chair, my mind spiraling. "Felicia, you've destroyed me. I'm literally ruined."

"Or," Felicia said, plucking a chip off the table with surgical precision, "he's into you and just needs some time. And you're over here doing mental gymnastics. It's not that deep."

I groaned. "You don't understand."

"Well, then you're really not gonna like when we talked about that day at the café."

"*The* day?"

She laughed at my misfortune. "He definitely had a thing for you, and he said that now he understands you just didn't want things to get messy. But at the time, he didn't see it that way. It felt like you snubbed him every chance you got, even though you were the one who had started flirting in the first place. That really threw him off, especially given the obvious mixed signals."

I gasped. "I barely flirted with him! He didn't even give me a chance to do my little hand trick," I said, offended.

"I should've told him he missed out, then."

Hearing myself clearly, I let out a nervous laugh bubble. "Not that hand trick!" I said, but a heavy weight had lifted off my shoulders. "The caressing thing, Fel."

We both burst out laughing, and for a moment, the tension in the room evaporated like steam from a kettle. Felicia leaned in, her eyes gleaming with mischief. "Honestly, I think the more you pushed him away, the more he wanted you. Can you think of anyone who's ever rejected him? *Hell no.* You were the one that got away, and that hurt him more than he's willing to admit."

I stood there, half-mortified, half-amused, and a tiny part of me wondered if maybe this whole thing could be salvaged or if I should cut my loses.

"Why me?" I groaned, pinching the bridge of my nose. But after the fourth time Felicia had repeated herself—albeit with a few slight variations—I finally felt it, like a soft tap on the head. Maybe she was right. She was right.

Felicia shrugged. "Because you're you. And let's face it, no one's ever told him to go to hell quite like you did. That probably left a mark."

"Lexi says men like a challenge," I mused, my brain doing mental gymnastics worthy of an Olympic medal. "And I was quite the challenge."

"Understatement of the century," Felicia said, rolling her eyes.

My brain was doing gymnastics, but still, the whole thing felt like a game of Who's Lying to Whom?

I flopped onto the couch, staring at the ceiling. "What if I'm lying to myself?"

Felicia tossed a throw pillow at me. "Then stop lying and go for him. Or don't. Either way, stop pacing. You're wearing a hole in the floor."

CHAPTER

NINE

THE NEXT MORNING, IN a desperate attempt to cheer me up (or at least stop me from Googling "how to erase someone from your memory"), Lexi, Felicia, and I went out for brunch. It wasn't the weekend, but Felicia had the day off, and after Claire's surprise early delivery turned the office into a biohazard zone (thanks to the amniotic waterfall incident), we were all granted an impromptu day off. Honestly, it was a blessing in disguise. After a night of tossing, turning, and dreaming about Eric (again), I needed a distraction. Preferably one involving carbs and mimosas.

"You're never going to believe what I just heard," Lexi announced, her grin so wide it could've been sponsored by Crest Whitestrips. We were seated at our usual table, surrounded by the comforting chaos of clinking cutlery and the scent of fresh gossip. I was already on my second mimosa

—nothing like a little liquid courage to drown out the existential dread—and Lexi was clearly on her third. Felicia? Well, I was still mad at her for the whole *Eric gave me a ride* debacle, so I refused to even glance at her drink count.

"Remember when we ran into Tegan at the Wynn Chanel?" Lexi asked, her eyes sparkling with the kind of mischief usually reserved for heist movies.

I groaned. Fucking Tegan. "Yes, though I'd rather not relive that particular nightmare over a perfectly good mimosa."

Felicia coughed into her napkin. Lexi, of course, noticed. "Okay, something's definitely going on with you two, but can you wait with the dramatics? This is *important*."

"Good, because nothing happened," Felicia muttered, and I rolled my eyes so hard I nearly gave myself a headache.

Lexi laughed, clearly savoring the drama. "Oh, this is too good," she said, practically vibrating with excitement. "Right. So, Heather called. You remember Heather, right?"

I nodded, because who could forget Heather? She was the woman who'd been swindled out of $100K by a trust-fund middle-aged man (TFMAM™) who promised her a penthouse and delivered a one-way ticket to Heartbreak Hotel.

Felicia chimed in, her tone dripping with faux sympathy. "Isn't she the one who paid for a down payment on a condo, and the TFMAM took the money and ran?"

Right, Felicia. She could remember that, but she couldn't remember to be a loyal friend to me?

Hmph.

"The very one," Lexi confirmed, grinning like a cat. "And guess where she's staying now with her newest TFMAM?"

I blinked, still deep in my bad mood and not ready for another round of nonsense. "The nursing home?"

Lexi nearly choked on her mimosa, her laughter bubbling over like a shaken champagne bottle. "Jesus, Eva. You're really in quite the mood," she said, nudging my shoulder playfully before taking another sip.

Felicia, meanwhile, delivered an eye-roll so dramatic it could've been choreographed by Beyoncé. "Okay, fine. Where is she staying, then?"

"None other than… the Nobu Villa!" Lexi practically squealed, her voice hitting a pitch usually reserved for dog whistles.

Felicia blinked, her mimosa hovering mid-sip. "So… she's rich again? Oh, wait. She's got another TFMAM. Never mind."

"Wait," I said, the gears in my brain finally grinding into motion.

"Yes, bitch, yes! The Nobu Villa!" Lexi was practically vibrating with excitement.

Felicia, still lost, took another sip of her mimosa. "Okay, I don't get it."

"The day we ran into Tegan at Chanel," I explained, my smile creeping back despite my best efforts, "she told us she was living at the Nobu Villa. As in *permanently*. She said she'd 'moved up' from the Wynn Villa to the Nobu Villa."

Felicia's jaw dropped. "Liar! Who does she think she is? Oprah's richer cousin?"

"Exactly!" Lexi said, her smugness dialed up to eleven. "Either she's lying—again—or Scott's lying to her. Personally, I don't know anyone who'd actually live in a $30K-a-night villa. And I know *rich*-rich people."

"$30K a night?" Felicia repeated, her voice rising an octave. "That's more than my gross net for a year!"

"Oh, sweetie," Lexi said, looking mortified for Felicia. "Want me to set you up—never mind. I just remembered you left me out to dry with Scott and Ty. Find your own bank transfer."

"I'd rather not. If I wanted to pretend I was an extra on

Heartbreakers, I'd pick Jen Love's brain, not yours," Felicia said, sipping her drink, shooting me a look.

Lexi ignored her, leaning in like she was about to drop the plot twist of the century. "Heather stayed there for three nights, and even that was excessive." She sat up straight. "Which is what?" She said, as if she were quizzing us.

"An investment," Felicia and I said in unison, our Lexi-trained brains finally syncing up.

"Exactly. So, if Tegan's claiming she lives there, she's either delusional or Scott's getting something out of it. Because that would be a *seizable* investment."

Felicia frowned, still not quite there. "But isn't Scott third-generation rich? Can't he afford $30K a night?"

"Sure, once in a while," Lexi said, her tone dripping with condescension. "But not even Charles would blow that kind of cash on a hotel room. You're missing the point."

Felicia froze, her mimosa forgotten as she tried to piece it together.

I sighed. "If Heather's staying at the Nobu Villa," I said, barely suppressing an eye-roll, "then Tegan can't be living there, can she?"

"Oh, shit," Felicia muttered, her mimosa glass pausing mid-air as the penny finally dropped.

"Exactly," Lexi said, her grin widening like she'd just won the lottery. "I asked Charles about it when Tegan mentioned the Nobu Villa, but he didn't even know Scott had moved out of the Wynn. So, either Scott's lying to him, or Charles is lying to me. And let's be real—Charles doesn't lie to me. If he did, he wouldn't get what he wants. And trust me, he *always* gets what he wants."

"Well, Tegan's a known liar," I said, my mind racing faster than a caffeinated squirrel. "So, it's pretty obvious who's full of it. The real question is why would she lie?"

"With Tegan, it's more like, why wouldn't she lie?" Felicia quipped, her tone dripping with sarcasm. "She's practically made a career out of it."

I couldn't help but smile. Felicia had a point. I'd been spiraling over this whole mess like it was the plot of a Netflix thriller, when really, it was just Tegan being Tegan.

"There's only one reason she'd lie," Lexi said, her voice suddenly serious.

"What's that?"

"Scott's not giving her the high-roller life he promised, but she has to keep up appearances. That's it. That's the reason."

"Oh," I said, the pieces clicking into place. "So, her little erotic-asphyxiation-first-date didn't land her the penthouse after all. But instead of admitting it, she's doubling down on the fantasy."

"Exactly," Lexi said, nodding like a proud professor. "And if she's lying about where she's staying, she's probably lying about everything else too, mind. It's all about the image for her. Being publicly rejected doesn't exactly scream 'I'm living my best life.'"

Felicia raised an eyebrow. "But isn't she still getting married?"

"As far as we know, yes," I said. "But who knows? Maybe she's lying about that too."

"Guess time will tell," Felicia said, shrugging like she'd just solved a crossword puzzle.

"Anyway," Lexi interjected, clearly bored with Tegan's theatrics, "what are you two hiding?"

"Oh, nothing," I said, my tone so innocent it could've been bottled and sold as spring water. "Just that Felicia took a ride from Eric yesterday, and they had a lot to say about me."

Lexi's eyes went wide, her mimosa sloshing dangerously close to the rim. "Spill it!" she demanded, her voice dropping to a conspiratorial whisper.

Felicia sighed dramatically, like she was about to recount the plot of a Shakespearean tragedy. By the time she finished, I turned to Lexi, silently begging for some kind of validation.

"That's it?" Lexi asked, sounding thoroughly unimpressed. "I thought you had something juicy."

"What do you mean? They spent the whole time talking about me and every little mistake I've ever made!"

"Eva, honey, this is brilliant news!" Lexi declared. "If anything, it means Eric's still mad about you. He's probably spent nights staring at that viral video, muttering, 'Why won't she love me?!' like a rom-com extra."

I slumped deeper into my chair, the ice in my mimosa melting like my resolve. "It's not about Eric," I muttered, though my voice wavered like a Wi-Fi signal in a storm. "It's Tegan. *Again*. She's like a human glitter grenade—every time I think I've swept up the mess, she explodes another layer."

Lexi snorted. "Oh please. You're not upset about Tegan. You're upset because Eric actually had the hots for you, and now you're stuck wondering if his rant with Felicia was secretly a love confession."

"At Chanel, she told me they slept together," I blurted, the words tumbling out like loose Skittles. "And now I don't know if *he's* lying or *she's* lying or if I'm just a delusional."

Lexi burst out laughing, nearly upending the avocado toast. "That's why you've been moping like someone canceled Christmas? Eva, everyone's slept with someone. Hell, if I was him, I'd sleep with as many people as I could a day! You can't judge Eric for having a past."

"It's not funny!" I hissed, though I could already feel my drama spiraling into ridiculous territory.

"Sweetie, if you're going to obsess over every guy Tegan's ever blinked at, you'll need a spreadsheet," Felicia drawled, sipping her mimosa like she was in a champagne ad. "Newsflash: Eric's not a virgin nun. Neither are you. *Shocking*, I know."

"I know that," I snapped, defensive. "But why lie? It's the lying that's—"

"—eating you alive?" Lexi finished, arching a brow. "Face it, Eva. You're a closet romantic. You're not mad he slept with Tegan—you're mad she got there first. Like she pirouetted into your meet-cute and stole your popcorn."

"Told you," Felicia sing-songed, swirling her drink.

Lexi leaned in, her tone softening. "Tegan's karma will come. Maybe her fake Nobu Villa will collapse into a koi pond. But you? You're letting her live rent-free in your head.

Evict her. Paint the walls. Host a rave."

I sighed, picking at my bread. "It's just… hard."

"Obviously," Felicia said, deadpan. "Hence the fourth mimosa."

Lexi's phone buzzed, and she gasped. "Oh! Brody just texted. Apparently, Eric's—"

"Enough about Eric," I said, buzzing at the thought of him.

"I know you've been mad at me," Felicia said, then tipped her mimosa all the way back. "But I have some more news you're probably not going to like."

The table froze. My stomach did a backflip worthy of Cirque du Soleil.

"What now?"

"Eric has a girlfriend.

I stared at my mimosa, suddenly wishing it were a margarita. A very large margarita.

"Great. Just great."

CHAPTER

TEN

"I DIDN'T WANT TO say anything yesterday because you were already so fired up," Felicia began, pausing with the theatrical flair, her mimosa lifted halfway to her lips. "But Eric was at the café. With someone. A girl someone, in case I wasn't clear."

My heart performed an Olympic-worthy dive straight into my stomach, but I plastered on a grin so forced it could've been held together with duct tape. I was embarrassed deep down, very deep down. Especially because I'd been making such a big deal about Tegan's gross lie about sleeping with Eric. Even if he hadn't slept with her, he was sleeping with someone else, so what did it matter to me.

"Oh?" I managed, swirling my drink like I didn't care. "Good for him. Maybe she'll teach him how to pronounce 'croissant' properly."

Lies. The word *someone* echoed in my head like a rogue ping-pong ball. *Someone* with better hair? *Someone* who didn't accidentally call him a "disgusting pig" in front of 5 million viewers? *Someone* who—

"Eva," Lexi cut in, her voice dripping with the subtlety of a sledgehammer, "you're doing that thing where you pretend you're fine, but your left eye is twitching like Morse code for 'I'm spiraling.'"

"I'm *fine*," I insisted, half for me, half for them. "What do I care about that? Eric and I are just rebuilding a very cracked friendship. That's all." But I chugged the rest of my mimosa.

Lexi snorted. "Right. And I'm the Duchess of Sussex."

"No, really. There's nothing between us and–"

Lexi wouldn't drop it, hanging on to every word like a candle fire. "Oh, stop it, Eva. You've never been a good liar, and I can see right through you."

Likewise, I couldn't stop it. "It's not that, Lexi. You just don't understand–"

"Oh, I get it, trust me. We all do." Lexi's voice softened, and for a second, she looked almost serious. "I hate Tegan probably more than you do. She's got everything I've ever wanted, and she got in like five minutes, while I've been working my butt off for years just to get anywhere close. So yeah, I get it."

Felicia, bless her soul, had had enough mimosas to think she was some sort of expert. "I hate Tegan, too," she slurred, her cheeks flushed from the unlimited champagne. "That bitch was so mean to Eric."

"Okay," I said, taking the last mimosa. "Slow down there, Felicia."

"The new girl looks like she drinks deadlifts for breakfast and pushups for dinner. She has this whole 'Muscles are life' vibe," Felicia said, waving her straw like a wand.

Lexi leaned in, her gaze sharp enough to slice through my facade. "Look, I know you're secretly drafting a PowerPoint with pros and cons and reasons Eric doesn't like you, but here's the tea: Tegan sucks, but it's no reason to let her win. You're letting her redecorate your brain like it's a Fixer-Upper episode."

I slumped, my defiant posture crumbling. "She lied," I muttered, the word tasting bitter. "About everything. Our friendship, Eric... everything."

Felicia, now hugging her empty mimosa flute like a teddy bear, hiccuped. "Also, New Girl? She could probably lift Eric over her head. Just saying."

"It's not about Eric!" I snapped, louder than intended, startling a nearby waiter into dropping a spoon.

Lexi arched a brow. "Sure. And I'm definitely not texting Brody to find out if Eric's single."

"Lexi—"

"Too late." She smirked, tapping her phone. "Sent a winky face. And a cactus emoji. For subtext."

I groaned, but secretly—terribly, pathetically—a flicker of hope ignited in my chest. Maybe Eric's *someone* was temporary. Maybe bridges could be rebuilt.

Or maybe I'd just order another mimosa.

The sunlight filtering through the studio windows was practically begging to be Instagrammed, but after my recent stint in the viral category, I'd rather not. Plus, my Downward Dog was making me cramp like crazy. Still, I clung to the delusion that yoga would fix my life. *Breathe in, Eva. Breathe out. Forget that Lexi said she'd slept with—stop it, Eva.*

By the time I collapsed into Savasana—or "Corpse Pose," which felt fitting after the emotional homicide of yesterday's brunch—my mind was racing faster than a greyhound chasing a sausage. *Let it go*, the instructor had purred. Sure, I'd "let go" of Tegan's betrayal, Eric's confusing—dimples, and the fact that my car's GPS still thought it was 2016. But letting go of the mortification that my friends had staged an intervention over bottomless mimosas? Tough.

"You're evolving, Eva," I muttered to myself, peeling my yoga mat off the floor. "New mantra: No more obsessing over men who bench-press refrigerators or women who make your life miserable."

But as I parked my seven-year-old car, the café loomed ahead like Mount Doom. *Live your damn life*, I ordered myself.

"Eva!" Felicia stage-whispered the moment I stumbled in, her eyes wide with urgency. "He's here."

My heart did a full gymnastics routine—backflip, dismount, face-plant—as I spotted Eric. Of course he was at *my* table. And of course he wasn't alone.

Next to him sat a woman who looked like she'd been carved from marble. Her biceps alone could've crushed a watermelon. Or my self-esteem. They were laughing at something—probably the tragic origin story of "Unhinged Café Girl"—but when she turned to me, her smile sharpened into a glare that screamed, "I eat girls like you for fun."

"Eva!" Eric waved, cheerful as a golden retriever who'd forgotten he'd once been called a "disgusting" on the internet—by me. "Join us! Your VIP tickets are here!" He patted the chair beside him like he was saving me a seat.

I forced a grin, silently cursing my luck. I'd half-hoped Felicia's mimosa-induced honesty had been mistaken, but of course, it hadn't.

I sat, unable to look away from General Nanisca sitting next to ~~my man~~ Eric. "Oh! Great! I'll just… pop these in my bag," I said, snatching the tickets like they were evidence in a heist. "Wouldn't want to interrupt your *chat*."

The woman arched a brow, her voice smooth as a protein shake. "Eric's told me so much about you. Sit down! Let's chat."

I was locked in a staring contest with—whatever this woman's name was—who'd somehow claimed Eric's bicep as her personal armrest. She was gorgeous. Radiant. Intimidating. I hated her instantly, with the fiery passion of a thousand suns.

"Has he," I mumbled, holding on to the seat beneath me lest I float off.

"Eva, this is Mindy Jones. She just joined the gym," Eric said, grinning—and as always, completely oblivious. Mindy

Jones. *Hate her*.

"It's *Misty* Mindy Jones," she corrected, her voice a smoky purr. "Because I come at you like a mist." She winked, extending a hand that could probably crush walnuts. Or dreams.

Shit.

I shook her hand, half-expecting her to flip me over her shoulder and demand reps. "Nice to meet you," I squeaked, sounding less confident café regular and more startled garden gnome.

"Why don't you sit a bit closer?" Misty patted the chair beside her, which was roughly the width of a postage stamp.

"I haven't even ordered yet—"

"I got your usual!" Felicia trilled, materializing like a rogue fairy godmother in an apron. She plonked my cortado and the mythical raspberry tart—finally back in stock—right in front of Misty Mindy. Traitor.

"Perfect," I muttered, shooting Felicia a glare that could melt steel.

Strike two, bitch.

"The service here is great," Misty Mindy remarked, sipping *my* coffee like she'd just claimed a throne. *Okay, she wants to fight.*

"She's actually my best friend," I said, sharper than intended. "So she knows what I like."

Misty Mindy laughed—a rich, velvety sound. "So, what's good, Eva?" She drawled my name like it was a trivia question she'd already aced.

"Torres," I snapped. "Eva Torres."

"So, what's good, Eva Torres?" she repeated, leaning in like a lioness.

"Uh... nothing. I just—"

Thankfully, Eric cut in. "Eva's a regular here," he said, blissfully oblivious to the tension. "I always see her on Saturday mornings after her Pilates class." He flashed a smile that should've been illegal, then stared at his hands like he'd said to much.

I sighed inwardly. If only he knew.

"It was yoga today," I said, straightening my spine like I hadn't spent half of Savasana plotting my escape. "But yes. Creature of habit."

Misty smirked, swirling her spoon in my stolen cortado. "Cute."

Cute. The word hung in the air like a bad perfume. Cute,

as in "adorably forgettable." Cute, as in "I'll bench-press your man while you downward dog."

Felicia, sensing imminent disaster, slid a second tart toward me with a nervous grin. A peace offering.

I took a savage bite.

Let the games begin.

"Routine's the foundation of civilization," Eric chimed in, clearly sensing my growing urge to bolt. "I'm a big fan. Huge fan, actually."

"Routine's boring. It's for people who think beige is a personality," Mindy shot back, smirking like she'd just invented spontaneity. "I prefer... chaos. Skydiving, midnight tacos, variety, spontaneity!" She leaned back, arms crossed over her biceps—which, frankly, looked like they could crack me in half.

"Sporadically, sure," I said, straightening my spine like I was auditioning for *Pride and Prejudice* corset role. "But I'll take my routine with a side of sanity, thanks. Some of us like knowing where our keys are."

"Sporadically," Mindy repeated, snorting like I'd quoted Shakespeare in pig Latin. "Did you binge-watch *Clueless* last night or something, Thesaurus Girl?"

I opened my mouth to volley back, but Eric—bless his

clueless soul—jumped in. "Our life is mostly routine, Mindy. Gym, eat, sleep, repeat." He took a bite of Felicia's Muscle Muffin, all protein, zero sugar.

Mindy's retort died as Brody burst in, jingling like a cowboy with a keychain addiction. Eric excused himself, leaving me alone with Human Wrecking Ball Barbie.

"So. Eva," she said, leaning in so close I could see my terrified reflection in her aviators. "I've heard all about you. And I've seen the video, too. Cute meltdown. Very… viral."

"Yeah, well, editing really is everything," I quipped, though my voice squeaked like a deflating balloon animal.

"Let's cut the crap." She slammed a hand on the table, rattling the sugar packets. "Stay away from Eric. You pull another little stunt like that, and you'll have me to deal with. He's a softie, but I'm not."

"Yeah, that was a misunderstanding," I said, voice almost wobbling.

"Well don't misunderstand this: Fuck with Eric, and I'll fuck you, got it?"

Oh, fantastic. "I'm not fucking with Eric. We're just—"

"Good," she cut in, crushing a protein bar wrapper like it was my soul. "Because if I hear one more whisper about you two, I'll make that viral video look like a TikTok unboxing.

And honey? I don't need followers to ruin your day."

"It wasn't planned, okay? That video was a misunderstanding," I blurted, my voice wobbling like a Jenga tower in an earthquake. My heart was pounding so hard I half-expected it to stage a jailbreak through my ribcage. Meanwhile, Mindy stood there, cool as a cucumber in a freezer. Bitch.

"I said, got it?"

"Got to go, Mindy," Eric interrupted, tapping her on the back like he was swatting a fly. He flashed his usual golden retriever grin, blissfully unaware of the emotional Chernobyl unfolding around him. "Back to training. Eva, good to see you again."

"Yeah, you too," I forced out, but I was thinking, *glad you're leaving.*

"Catch you later, Eva," Mindy purred, her tone dripping with enough menace to make a Bond villain jealous. Her words sent a chill down my spine that no amount of yoga breathing could fix.

The second they were out the door, Felicia materialized like a caffeine-fueled ninja. "What the hell was that about?"

"I have no idea," I muttered, clutching my cortado like it was a lifeline. "She hates me for no reason."

"Dammit, Eva. She's terrifying. What are we supposed to do?"

"She hates *me*, not you," I said, trying to sound reassuring. "You're probably safe."

"That's where you're wrong," Felicia shot back, her hands on her hips to show she meant it. "If she's got a problem with you, she's got a problem with me."

I stared at her, awestruck. Felicia, who once cried because the café ran out of oat milk, was ready to throw down with a woman who looked like she could bench-press a minivan.

"I've been so mad at you for no reason," I admitted, guilt washing over me like a rogue wave. "You really are my best friend."

"Of course I am, silly," Felicia said, bumping my shoulder. "And if that bitch wants to come for you, she's gotta come for me too. I don't care how scary she is; I'll fight back."

"Let's just hope she doesn't feel like kicking anyone's ass, Felicia," I said, half-laughing, half-dreading the mental image of Misty Mindy in full combat mode.

CHAPTER

ELEVEN

"THE NEW GIRL IS such a nightmare," Lexi declared, murdering her salad with a fork, the poor thing hadn't stood a chance. We were crammed at our usual table at Olive Garden—the one that wobbled like a drunk flamingo. Our lunchtime ritual today was dissecting workplace scandals like we were hosting a true-crime podcast. This week's episode: The Case of the Glacial Temp.

"I've deployed five peace offerings," Lexi hissed, ticking them off on her fingers. "A coffee, a Post-it compliment, a 'You've got spinach in your teeth' heads-up—nothing. She looked at me like I'd asked her to donate a kidney to a stranger."

"Maybe she's just nervous?" I ventured, though privately I agreed. She'd iced me out too, and all I'd done was smile at her in the break room. (Note to self: Smiling is now a war crime.) Still, I clung to optimism. She was only here temporarily, filling in for Claire—our mindful whisperer, lunchtime therapist, and the only person who knew how to fix the printer.

"I miss Claire," I sighed, poking my endless pasta like it might confess secrets.

"Same," Lexi said, already dialing. "Quick, I need a baby Ethan serotonin hit before I start stress-eating HR's 'motivational' mints."

Claire answered, her hair in a I've-birthed-a-human topknot, baby Ethan gurgling in the background like a tiny, sleep-deprived CEO. "How's the replacement?" she asked, though her eyes were glazed in that I've-been-awake-for-days way.

"Oh, she's adjusting," I said, as Lexi mimed dramatic gagging.

"She's a soulless desk goblin," Lexi clarified cheerfully. "But don't worry—we'll Stockholm Syndrome her into liking us by Friday."

Claire snorted, panning the camera to Ethan, who was making a face that screamed "more milk, mommy!" "Miss you both," she yawned. "But honestly, this is more sleep than I got during Spring Break 2019. Baby's a menace, though, if he doesn't get his boob on time."

"You've got this," Lexi said, baby fever chills showing through her *goo goo gaga face*. "I want to smell his little baby head! Cutie!"

"Tell me more about this replacement."

"She's no Claire, I'll say that," Lexi said, grinning. "Point is, New Girl'll crack. They always do."

Claire chuckled, eyelids drooping. "Just send her baby spam—she'll run away from that, to be sure. And maybe hide all the staplers until I'm back."

"Deal," Lexi said, holding her lemonade to cheer. "To Claire, Ethan, and surviving the office dumpster fire. And to New Girl—may she develop a sudden passion for silent meditation retreats."

Claire jumped in, her voice dripping with mock solemnity. "Let's be real, Lexi, you were a bit of a territorial nightmare when we first met Eva. Admit it."

"Excuse me!" Lexi gasped, clutching her chest like she'd been accused of treason. "I was protective of our office friendships. There's a difference."

"Protective?" I snorted. "You practically growled at me every time I walked into the break room. I thought you were going to start marking your territory with Post-its."

"Okay, fine," Lexi relented, throwing her hands up. "Maybe I was a little territorial. But come on, Eva, you weren't exactly sunshine and rainbows either. You had that whole 'I'm-too-cool-for-this-place' vibe going on."

"I did not!" I protested, though Claire was already nodding in agreement.

"It took you a while to warm up," Claire said diplomatically, her tone the verbal equivalent of patting a small, angry dog on the head.

"I was nice!" I insisted, but they'd already moved on, cooing over baby Ethan's latest noises like he'd just recited Shakespeare. Honestly, he still looked like a tiny, wrinkled alien to me, but I kept that thought to myself. Claire had enough on her plate without me insulting her offspring. Besides, my niece Rubi had looked like a potato when she was born, and now she was the most adorable toddler on the planet. Newborns are just an acquired taste.

Lexi, ever the master of abrupt topic changes, suddenly blurted, "You'll never guess what happened yesterday."

"Charles finally agreed to marry you without a prenup?" I said sweetly, knowing full well that was Lexi's ultimate fantasy—and also because I was still a tiny bit salty about her thinking I was the office ice queen when we first met.

"Ha. Ha. Very funny," Lexi deadpanned. "No, Tegan

Anderson and Scott Van Hoff sent out *another* round of wedding invitations. They're changing the date, the venue, the whole thing. Charles and I got one."

"No way," I said, my jaw dropping. Tegan always managed to land on her feet, no matter how ridiculous the situation. "What's the rush? Is she worried Scott's going to wake up one day and realize he's marrying a human garbage disposal?"

"Exactly," Claire chimed in, nodding sagely. "She's probably trying to lock him down before he changes his mind."

"That's what I thought at first," Lexi said, tapping her chin like a detective solving a mystery. "But something feels off. The wedding's next week. *Next week*. Who plans a wedding that fast? Unless..."

"She's pregnant," I finished, the words tumbling out before I could stop them. "I mean, it's Tegan. If there's money involved, she'd have a baby with a cactus if it came with a trust fund."

"Felicia's cousin pulled off a shotgun wedding in three days," Claire added, as if this were a perfectly normal thing to do. "So it's not impossible."

"Scott's about as emotionally invested as a Roomba," Lexi declared. "He's got kids sprinkled across the globe like confetti. All he does is toss money at them from his trust fund—which, let's be honest, is basically a human ATM with a yacht habit."

"Then why the Vegas sprint?" I asked, nibbling a piece of bread.

Claire chimed in, adjusting Ethan's tiny hat, which he'd already flung off twice. "Maybe she's the one with cold feet. You can't mistake pegging and a choking for true love, right? That's like calling a microwave dinner gourmet."

"I forgot about the pegging!" I shuddered, nearly dropping my lemonade. "And Scott's hands choking Tegan— they look like they've been marinating in a toolbox since the Clinton administration. Imagine those trying to—"

"Nope," Claire cut in, laughing so hard Ethan jerked, his gurgles morphing into a tiny opera of indignation. "And scene, ladies! Nap time's over. Duty calls." She waved goodbye, leaving Lexi and me to dissect Tegan's latest dramedy.

"Maybe she's racing to altar-hop before Scott notices she's allergic to good sense and taking things slow," Lexi mused. "Or she's just gaslighting herself into believing hashtag-wedding-bliss."

"Instagram recon?" I suggested, leaning over. "Let's

cyber-stalk her into confessing."

Tegan's feed was a masterclass in faux-joy: wind-machine hair, legs for days, and a diamond so massive it could've anchored the Titanic. "She's filtered to oblivion," Lexi snorted. "That ring's basically a paperweight for the Hope Diamond."

"And Vegas?!" I squawked. "She could marry on a private moon, but she picks the neon chapel of what-happens-here-stays-here? Why?"

"Scott's fifth wedding jitters?" Lexi shrugged. "Or he's saving his trust fund for something sensible, like a gold-plated helicopter."

We dissolved into giggles, the absurdity wrapping around us like a warm, ridiculous blanket. "Tegan's playing 4D chess with confetti cannons," I sighed. "And we're just here for the popcorn."

"Speaking of Eric," Lexi said, leaning across the table with the subtlety of a wrecking ball, "how's that fine man doing?"

"We were *not* talking about Eric," I said, leaning on my chair. The last thing I wanted to do was talk about Eric and his new girlfriend. "Let's talk about Brody instead. You know, the man you're actually dating?"

Lexi's face did that thing it always did when Brody came up—like someone had flipped a switch and turned her into a human glow stick. "There's not much to say," she said, waving a hand like she was swatting away a fly. "He's busy, I'm busy, but we make it work. And honestly, the best part is how much it *kills* Charles."

"Ah, the prenup revenge plot thickens."

"Exactly," Lexi said, her grin widening. "If Charles is going to dangle a prenup over my head like it's the Holy Grail, then I'm going to dangle Brody Jensen in front of his face. Now every time Charles watches UFC, he has to sit there and think, *That's the guy Lexi's dating.* It's delicious."

"Sure, Lexi," I said, trying to sound supportive but failing miserably. "Because nothing says healthy relationship like using a professional fighter to torture your sugar daddy."

"Oh, come on," Lexi said, tossing her napkin at me. "It's not like I'm marrying Brody. He's fun, sure. The conversations are actually fun—unlike Charles, who once spent an entire dinner explaining the tax benefits of offshore accounts. But Brody's future is too unpredictable. He's got to win a lot of fights to make it big, and I need stability. Charles is a sure thing."

"Except for the whole prenup thing," I couldn't resist adding.

"Yes, Eva," Lexi said, glaring at me. "Except for the prenup. Thank you for never letting me forget."

The server arrived with our check, complete with a smiley face.

"Anyway," Lexi said, stabbing the air with her fork, "don't think you're getting out of the Eric question. Spill."

"There's nothing to spill," I said, suddenly very interested in the smiley face. "He invited me to his fight, and I said I'd go. That's it."

"Wait, he got a fight?" Lexi's eyes widened like I'd just announced I'd won the lottery.

"Yeah," I admitted reluctantly. "It's in May."

"*May*?" Lexi practically shrieked. "Eva, that's huge! That viral video must've worked in his favor. I told you it would!"

"Yes, yes, you're a genius," I said, rolling my eyes again. "But it's just a fight. No big deal."

"No big deal?" Lexi repeated, her voice dripping with sarcasm. "Eva, he invited *you*. That's basically the romantic equivalent of a knight asking you to his jousting tournament!"

"Oh, for God's sake," I muttered, but Lexi was already grinning like she'd just won the prenup war.

"Holy shit," Lexi said, excitement dripping from her pores. She downed the last of her drink in one go, which, frankly, was impressive. "Brody didn't say a word about a fight in May. That's, like, next month."

"Oh, and by the way, I met his new girlfriend."

"Eric doesn't exactly have a type, does he?" Lexi chuckled, clearly amused by her own observation. I, however, was not laughing. "Honestly, I didn't think they were actually a thing. I figured Felicia was just being Felicia—you know, jumping to conclusions like she's in the Olympic long-jump finals. But Brody says Eric isn't labeling anything. It's all up in the air."

"But she exists and you *knew* about her," I pointed out, trying to keep the hurt out of my voice. It wasn't that I expected Lexi to report every detail of Eric's life to me, but it stung that she hadn't mentioned Misty Mindy sooner. Especially since I'd spent the last few months nursing a hopeless crush on him. Lexi was usually a solid friend, but she had her moments. Then again, monogamy wasn't exactly her strong suit, so maybe I shouldn't have been surprised.

"I've seen her around," Lexi said with a shrug. "She's new to the gym. Always hanging onto Eric like he's a life raft in the middle of the ocean. But I didn't think they were actually dating. There are other girls who'd jump at the chance to be with him, you know."

Great. So there's more than one. No wonder she didn't tell me.

"She's... protective," I admitted, remembering how Mindy had looked at me. "It was kind of weird."

"She's definitely intense," Lexi said, nodding sagely. "Probably all the extra testosterone."

I gasped, then burst out laughing. "Lexi, that's not how it works."

"Oh, come on," she said, grinning. "You have to admit, she's got to be on *something* to look that buff. That's not natural."

"Isn't that illegal in the UFC?" I asked, suddenly feeling like an expert in sports regulations. "It's illegal in the Olympics, right?"

"Look at you, Miss Wikipedia," Lexi teased. "Honestly, I don't know. All I can tell you is that she's a little too strong for my liking. Like, if she arm-wrestled me, I'd probably lose an arm."

"She's tough, sure," I said, and trying to sound nonchalant, I told her all about our meeting. "A bit abrasive, but nothing I can't handle."

"Are you kidding me, Eva?" Lexi's eyes widened. "She

basically threatened you! And she's a scrapper. I wouldn't mess with her. I've known girls like that my whole life—they're everywhere in the stripper scene, and my mom always told me to steer clear. They don't fear anything. You better watch your back. You don't know the world she's from."

"Oh, come on," I said, crossing my arms defensively. "I come from immigrant parents and limited resources. I'm not exactly quaking in my boots over Misty Mindy. She's just judging me because of that stupid video."

"The video was a mess," Lexi admitted. "But let's be real—it also kind of worked out in the end. Eric's got more attention now than he's ever had. And, hate to break it to you, but you kinda helped make that happen."

I cringed. "I didn't *do* anything." Except, well, maybe I did. But not in the way Lexi meant.

"As bad as it sounds, you kinda did," Lexi said, shrugging. "And Eric knows it. So does Mindy. She's probably just jealous because Eric obviously has a thing for you, and you two are, like, polar opposites. Plus, you're the one who accidentally turbocharged his career."

"I don't think that's it," I said, though a tiny part of me wondered if Lexi was right.

"Hey, girl!" Felicia's voice cut through the air as she climbed into my car, tossing her apron into the back seat like it was a frisbee. I hated when she did that—she'd forget it back there, and it would start to smell like old coffee and regret. But today, she brought one of her famous raspberry tarts, so I let it slide. The tart was a sign. The viral video drama was finally dying down enough for there to be leftovers, and that alone was enough to lift my mood.

I took a deep breath, even though the heat in the car was borderline unbearable. "What's the gossip today?" I asked, grinning.

Felicia raised an eyebrow. "Since when do you ask *me* for gossip? You're the one bringing the juiciest stuff these days."

"Fine," I said, steering the car toward home. "Tegan's getting married."

"I already knew that," Felicia said, waving a hand dismissively. "Give me something better."

"Okay, how about this—she's getting hitched *next week*."

Felicia's eyes went so wide I thought they might pop out of her head. "*What?*"

I smirked, enjoying her reaction. "Yep."

"I wonder what sexual favor she pulled this time to get everything moved up so fast," Felicia said, her tone dripping with sarcasm.

"Lexi didn't say," I replied, stealing a bite of the tart while we waited at a red light. "Or maybe she's done everything at this point."

Felicia snorted. "So, what's new at the café?" I asked, trying to sound casual.

She looked out the window, suddenly very interested in the passing scenery. "Nothing much. Misty ordered a latte for herself and a cappuccino... so..." She let the sentence hang there like a cliffhanger.

"Right," I said, taking another bite of the tart before the light turned green. Eric's go-to drink was a cappuccino. "Our lives couldn't get any more interesting, could they?"

We both burst out laughing, the kind of laugh that makes your stomach hurt and your cheeks ache. And as we drove home, I couldn't help but think that, despite the chaos, life was still pretty good.

CHAPTER

TWELVE

SPRING SHOWERS, IT TURNS out, are the great equalizer. Even the rich and fabulous aren't immune. Just ask Tegan.

It was Tegan's wedding weekend, and I was hiding in my apartment with the curtains open to nature's chaos, wearing socks that could double as sleeping bags.

Let it be said: Spring storms in the desert are God's way of reminding even *Tegan Van Fancypants* that she's not above a good old-fashioned soaking. Her hastily rescheduled wedding? Now a monsoon-themed disaster, complete with wind that's howling like a scorned ex at a karaoke bar. Meanwhile, I'm cozied up with Felicia's brown butter cookies, which are basically edible Xanax. (Note: Must patent that phrase.)

Felicia, ever the wizard of comfort food, had declared today a "no-pants, no-problems" kind of day. Her chocolate chip cookies smelled like a hug from your grandma—if your grandma were a French pastry chef with a slight butter addiction. The aroma alone was so nostalgic it almost made me weep. Or maybe that was the guilt from my earlier meltdown over… well, *everything*.

Outside, the sky was throwing a tantrum worthy of a true desert storm. Rain lashed the windows, and the valley looked like it'd been slapped through a car wash. But inside? Pure *coziness*. The apartment was a fortress of flaky pastries and mismatched mugs, where even the air felt like a weighted blanket.

Tegan, of course, was out there somewhere, probably reciting vows through a megaphone while her hair extensions whipped around like Medusa's snakes. No prenup, naturally. The woman could negotiate a peace treaty in stilettos. (Translation: If the storm doesn't drown her, the tabloids will. Cheers, Mother Nature.)

You'd think I'd be immune to Tegan's victories by now. Like, *oh, Tegan got her way again? Shocking. Post a story*. But no. Every time she wins, it's like someone's rubbing lemon juice on a paper cut. And not even a fancy organic lemon— just the cheap, waxy kind from the dollar store.

Still, I couldn't help but feel a tiny flicker of satisfaction knowing the storm was ruining her "perfect" wedding. Mother Nature: 1, Tegan: 0.

Felicia, ever the voice of reason (and butter), broke the silence. "These cookies are to die for," she said, taking a bite so dramatic it could've been in an A24 piece. "What's Lexi saying? Is she still at the wedding?"

I glanced at my phone, which was suspiciously quiet. "No updates. Last I heard, the storm's been brutal, and half the guests bailed. Lexi's there, though. Eric's not."

(Side note: Tegan had personally hand-delivered Eric's invite after rescheduling the wedding. Subtle, right? Like, *Hey, remember me? The one who got away? Anyway, here's a save-the-date for my shotgun wedding to a guy who can buy UFC twice over.*")

Felicia nodded, her expression a mix of wisdom and cookie-induced bliss. "Scott and Charles are tight. Lexi wouldn't miss this, especially with her whole no-prenup fantasy. But Eric? No way. He hates Tegan more than I hate decaf."

She wasn't wrong. Lexi had been playing the long game with Charles lately, and I wasn't sure if it was love, strategy, or some unholy combination of both. Tegan, meanwhile, was out there making power moves like she was auditioning for

Heartbreakers. Lexi's presence at the wedding wasn't just about showing support—it was chess, not checkers.

(Question: Is Lexi there for the gossip, or is this another favor for Charles? Answer: Yes.)

I sat on the couch, surrounded by cookie crumbs and a growing sense of schadenfreude.

Let's be real: Lexi's whole "favors for a TFMAM" (That Fancy Man About Town, jk! Trust Fund Middle-Aged Man, more like it) routine sounded about as glamorous as being a mannequin at a Diddy party. According to her, it was all about being arm candy at stuffy galas and smiling through painfully dull conversations about hedge funds and yacht taxes. Charles, she claimed, cared more about his public image than anything else—though, honestly, their "dates" sounded less like romance and more like an exchange as old as time.

Still, I never pressed her on it. Lexi was my friend, and if playing the part of Charles's polished plus-one got her the Porsche, the lifestyle, and the Instagram clout, who was I to judge? Besides, I'd mastered the art of nodding along while silently questioning everything. It's a skill, really.

My phone buzzed, snapping me out of my thoughts. "It's Lexi!" I said. "She sent a picture. Prepare yourself."

Felicia leaned in, her eyes narrowing as the image loaded.

"Wait. *That's* Tegan's wedding decor? Are we looking at the same photo? Those centerpieces look like they were cobbled together from a clearance bin at a craft store. And the flowers—oh my god, did they raid a gas station bouquet sale?"

I couldn't help but laugh. "There's no way Tegan's okay with this. You know how she is—everything has to be perfect. This is not that."

Tegan had always been the poster child for more is more. Designer labels, exclusive handbags, the kind of Instagram aesthetic that made you question your life choices. But since cozying up to Scott and his old-money crowd, she'd been trying to rebrand herself as the epitome of understated elegance. This wedding, though? It was giving *discount chic*.

(Mental image: Tegan, seething in a couture gown, surrounded by dollar-store carnations. Poetic justice, really.)

"This," Felicia said, gesturing at Lexi's latest photo, "is what happens when you try to plan a wedding in, like, three business days. It's giving panic mode."

The picture was… well, it was something. The reception, originally meant to be a glamorous outdoor affair, had been crammed indoors thanks to the storm. The result? A venue that looked like it had been decorated by someone who'd just binge-watched *Say Yes to the Dress* and thought, *I can do that*.

Spoiler: They could not.

(Note: Felicia's cousin's wedding, held in a condemned casino, was *still* classier. Let that sink in.)

"Let's check her socials," Felicia said, already scrolling with the intensity of a detective on a caffeine high. Then she gasped. "That bitch blocked me."

I shrugged, trying to play it cool. "She blocked me a long time ago. Welcome to the club."

Felicia groaned. "Guess we're relying on Lexi for the tea. This is better than reality TV."

The rest of the evening turned into a live commentary session, with every ping from Lexi sending us into a frenzy. The more photos we saw, the clearer it became: this wedding was rushed. Like, eloped-in-Vegas-but-forgot-the-Elvis-impersonator rushed. The decor was bargain-bin chic, the flowers looked like they'd been plucked from a roadside ditch, and the whole thing screamed "last-minute desperation."

"Didn't Lexi say Scott's family has, like, third-generation money?" Felicia asked, her eyes narrowing like she'd just spotted a clue in a murder mystery.

I nodded. "Yeah, old money. The kind that buys yachts and private islands."

Felicia's mind was clearly racing. "Something's off. Tegan's not exactly a spring chicken, and Scott's hands look like they've been through a war. Why the rush? Why the budget decor? This doesn't add up."

Felicia was onto something, and I knew that look. When she got that glint in her eye, it either meant she was about to uncover a scandal or accidentally burn the cookies. Given the subject matter, I was rooting for the former.

"Yeah, Lexi said his family's loaded. Like, old money, private jet, summer-in-the-Hamptons loaded," I replied, trying to ignore the memory of Scott sitting front-row at the club, watching me dance like I was part of some bizarre performance art piece.

Felicia squinted at the photos again, her brow furrowing like she was solving a math problem. "Well, you'd never know it from this wedding. I mean, this is sad. Do you think Scott's embarrassed? People with that kind of money usually go full *Great Gatsby* for their weddings."

I shrugged, trying to give Scott the benefit of the doubt. "Maybe he's just… low-key? Not into the whole showy thing?"

Felicia snorted. "Yeah, and maybe Tegan's secretly a nun. I'm Googling him."

And just like that, Felicia was off, her fingers flying across her phone like she was hacking into the Pentagon. Within minutes, we were knee-deep in a rabbit hole of articles, interviews, and gossip columns. Turns out, Scott Van Hoff wasn't the humble, unassuming guy I'd briefly imagined. Nope. He was the kind of guy who bought yachts on a whim and named them after himself.

(Side note: His yacht is literally called *The Scott Van Hoff*. Subtlety is not his strong suit.)

"So why the hell would he marry Tegan in a rush with… this?" I asked, gesturing at the photos of the sad centerpieces and wilted flowers. "It doesn't add up."

Felicia froze mid-scroll, her eyes widening. "Hold up," she said, her voice dripping with intrigue. "This article says Scott's mom and stepdad aren't coming to the wedding. They're, like, boycotting it. And they're calling Tegan a 'socialite.'"

"Socialite my ass," I spat, leaning in, practically climbing over Felicia to see the screen. The article, published just days before the wedding, claimed Scott's family was skipping the big day due to "financial and romantic disagreements."

"Financial and romantic disagreements?" I repeated, my brain working overtime. "What does that even mean? Did Tegan max out his credit card? Or is there something else going on?"

Felicia's eyes gleamed. "Oh, there's definitely something else going on. And I'm going to find out what."

Felicia let out a low whistle, the kind that usually precedes a bombshell. "His parents have to be, what, late eighties? Maybe nineties? If they're not showing up, this is serious." She paused, her eyes widening like she'd just cracked the Da Vinci Code. "Wait… what if they cut him off? What if that's why this wedding looks like it was planned by a hungover college student?"

I frowned, trying to piece it together. "I mean, Scott's gotta be in his sixties. Wouldn't he have access to his trust fund by now? Or is this some *Succession*-level family drama?"

Felicia shrugged, her curiosity now fully ignited. "Who knows? But if he's got the cash, why settle for this? It doesn't add up."

We sat in silence for a moment, both of us mentally flipping through the possibilities. The more we thought about it, the clearer it became: this wasn't just a rushed wedding. This was a statement. And whatever was going on behind the scenes, it was clearly bigger than Tegan and Scott.

"Besides," Felicia added, "why would Tegan marry him if there was no money? You know she did her homework. That woman's got a spreadsheet for everything."

"Well, she certainly spread—"

"Eva!"

Just as I was about to take another bite of cookie, my phone pinged. It was Lexi. She'd sent a photo of Tegan in her wedding dress.

I froze.

She looked stunning. Like, stop-traffic, break-the-internet stunning. The dress was clearly bespoke, all flowing silk and intricate lace, and it fit her like it had been sewn onto her body.

"Wow," I said, my voice barely above a whisper. "So much for the cheap wedding."

Felicia let out a low whistle. "Okay, maybe we were a little off the mark."

It wasn't that I *wanted* Tegan to lose—okay, maybe I did a little—but seeing her win *again* was like salt in a wound I thought had healed. The dress was flawless, the venue might've been a disaster, but Tegan? She was radiant. And I hated how much it stung.

"Why didn't we think of going after Scott for your revenge plot against Tegan?" Felicia asked, her tone half-serious.

I laughed, shaking my head. "Hell no. Eric was way

easier. And besides, it's too late for that now."

"Fucking Tegan," Felicia muttered, shoving another cookie into her mouth.

"Fucking Tegan," I echoed.

CHAPTER

THIRTEEN

I PARKED MY CAR outside the café, the spring heat clinging to the air like a clingy ex. Cranked up Sabrina Carpenter's latest bop as she begged some doofus to *please don't embarrass her*—and honestly, same, Sabrina. Same. I hadn't dated anyone since the Obama administration, but the song's vibe? Spot-on. A little drama, a little chaos—why not? And after dissecting Tegan's wedding of the *minute* with Lexi, I was primed to dish the dirt with Felicia. Mocking Tegan's life choices was practically a hobby at this point. More like therapy.

But then, of course, the universe decided to humble me.

Misty Mindy burst out of the café like she'd just won *The Price Is Right*, all biceps and bravado, laughing like she'd invented happiness. And trailing beside her? Eric Mann.

Great. Just fucking great.

I'd spent months perfecting the art of *not* wanting him—between my sheets, that is—but seeing him paired with Buff Barbie still pinched. Only I didn't care. *Obviously*.

He spotted my car and waved, all easy charm and dimples. I waved back, putting far too much effort into looking casually disinterested. (Note to self: Practice "casual indifference" in the mirror later. Maybe while eating ice cream for my troubles.)

The heat was killing me more than the slight jealousy was, and I texted Felicia: "Where are you? Dying. Heat. Cortado. Iced."

No reply. Typical. With Sabrina's song wrapping up, I gave up and trudged inside, praying Felicia had already conjured my iced cortado. The café's AC hit me like a hug from a snowman.

And then I saw him.

Brody. At *my* table. The one by the window with the wobbly leg and the faint coffee-stain Rorschach test. Brody Jensen, who usually treats cafés like a Tinder swipe—get in, get coffee, get out—was *lingering*. Slouched in the chair, eyes glued to his phone like he was decoding the meaning of life. Or, more likely, a UFC highlights reel.

Felicia materialized beside me, thrusting my cortado into my hand. But her eyes darted to Brody, then back to me, her eyebrow arching.

I followed her gaze back to all-muscles-no-brain Brody (Lexi said, not me), and there he was—still fused to his phone, still lingering. "Lexi," Felicia mouthed, her eyes widening with a mix of pity and a little fear. My heart did a little sad flop. Poor Brody. Bless his clueless soul.

Let's be real. Lexi's life "plan" was about as subtle as a disco ball in a library. We all knew Brody was just her emotional placeholder—a human speed bump until Charles crawled back, prenup-free and groveling. But seeing him camped out there, scrolling like his phone might suddenly flash *Lexi Loves You!* in neon? Tragic. The kind of tragic that makes you want to buy him a pint and a self-help book.

Honestly, it was like watching a golden retriever wait outside an empty house. *She's not coming, buddy*. But try telling him that. And why does no one warn these poor guys? "Sweetie, she's using you as an envy-inducing plot point. But bright side, your biceps are lovely."

Felicia shot me a look that screamed, "Should we toss him a life raft?" But what could we do? Some lessons, like never trust a woman who says 'monogamy is bourgeois,' you just have to learn the hard way.

I plopped into the table opposite Brody, doing my best impression of a chill café-goer—which, given the circumstances, was like trying to sip tea during an earthquake. Brody, usually the poster boy for nonchalance, sat hunched like a thundercloud in gym shorts. His shoulders were tighter than Felicia's apron strings, and his jaw looked like it was chewing on a lemon. *Yikes.*

Felicia swooped in, her smile wobbling like a Jenga tower. "Shane's late again and I can't leave, so… surprise!" She slid a strawberry-pistachio tart onto the table. "Strawberry and sablé crust. You're welcome."

My inner dessert critic screamed, "Yes, please!" One bite, and I was transported. The tart was a masterpiece—flaky, sweet, and probably illegal in some countries. Forget viral videos; this crust alone could've sparked a TikTok cult. I was mid-moan (the polite, pastry-related kind) when—

Scraaaaaape.

Brody's chair screamed like a banshee as he shot up, phone in hand, eyes blazing. "I don't care, Lexi! Come now, or I'll call that fat bastard you've been seeing. I'll tell him everything, don't try me!"

Felicia dropped her tray. A spoon clattered to the floor. The café's espresso machine chose that moment to hiss like a startled cat.

Oh, fuck. Brody had officially gone from "mysterious UFC hottie" to "soap opera villain." I froze, tart crumbs on my lip.

Felicia mouthed "WTF" with her entire face. I shrugged, because what do you do when a human grenade starts throwing threats? Brody's fists were clenched, his voice cracking like a teen at a BTS concert. This wasn't anger—it was a meltdown. And we were front-row spectators.

"Your little friends are here," he barked, jabbing a finger at us. "I'll use them and make another viral video. Let's see how you like that. I don't care about your stupid rules anymore."

Felicia turned sheet-white. I, meanwhile, contemplated hiding under the table. Brody wasn't just pushed too far— he'd pole-vaulted over the edge. The man now looked ready to flip a table. My favorite table.

"Right," Felicia whispered, clutching her apron like a security blanket. "Shane's definitely fired."

I nodded, eyeing the exit.

Felicia frantically motioned for me to join her behind the counter. I didn't need a second invitation. Brody wasn't just angry—he was unpredictable. And when the unpredictable person in question is a UFC fighter who could probably bench-press a small car, you don't stick around to ask questions.

I abandoned my iced cortado and the strawberry-pistachio tart (RIP, my sweet, sweet distraction) and scurried behind the counter. My heart was pounding so loudly I was half-convinced Brody could hear it.

He let out a low chuckle that sounded like a distant thunderstorm—equal parts thrilling and terrifying. "Now they're scared of me," he said, his voice a mix of amusement and something darker. His eyes locked onto ours, his tone dropped to a growl. "Relax. I'm not going to hurt you. I'm just making a point. So stop acting like you're in danger, because you're not."

(Translation: You're not in danger… but also, maybe you are?)

His words were supposed to be comforting, but they landed with all the warmth of a wet sock. If anything, they felt more like a threat wrapped in a riddle. I swallowed hard, wishing I had Eric's number—or, honestly, anyone's number. *Misty Mindy?* She could take him, right?

Felicia's hand found mine, and I gripped it like it was the last lifeboat on the *Titanic*. We huddled behind the counter, trying to steady our breathing. My eyes darted to the pastry display—rows of tarts and cakes glistening under the lights like edible shields. *If it comes to it,* I thought, *I'm throwing the sablé crust first.*

Felicia's grip loosened slightly as she scanned the counter, her mind clearly racing through the same absurd scenarios as mine. Brody was still on the phone, his voice quieter now but no less intense. His gaze flicked toward us, and I swear I felt the temperature drop.

(Side note: If looks could kill, we'd be in the freezer section.)

And then it hit me.

My phone.

I fumbled for it, my hands trembling like I'd mainlined six espressos. Scrolling through Instagram, I found Eric's message from earlier. My fingers flew across the screen, typing out a desperate plea for help, typos included.

Please don't be training. Please don't let Misty Mindy see this. Please, please, please.

Felicia peeked over my shoulder, her tense shoulders relaxing a fraction when she saw what I was doing. "Thank god for DMs," she muttered under her breath.

"Let's just pray he gets it before this turns into *Fight Club: Café Edition*," I whispered back, the words feeling like a fragile prayer.

The minutes dragged by like they were wading through

molasses. Brody was still glued to his phone, his voice low but crackling with tension. Every so often, his fist would slam onto the table, rattling the syrup bottles and making me jump like a cat who'd just seen a cucumber. It was like watching a pressure cooker about to explode—if the pressure cooker was a six-foot-something UFC fighter with the emotional regulation of a hangry toddler.

I'd texted Lexi, because *where was she?* This was her mess, wasn't it? All I got back was a cold, unfeeling read receipt. She knew what was happening, but whether she was racing to the rescue or already drafting her "Sorry, not sorry" text was anyone's guess.

The knot in my stomach tightened. Brody wasn't backing down, and neither was I, but my patience was wearing thinner than Felicia's last batch of puff pastry. I was about to dial 911 (or, let's be real, Eric again) when—

Jingle.

The café door swung open, and there he was.

Eric.

My knight in—slightly sweaty gym gear.

"Eva, what's going on?" he asked, his voice slicing through the tension like a hot knife through butter. His eyes darted to Brody, who was still mid-rant, his face red and his fists clenched like he was auditioning for *Rocky VII: Emotional Breakdown.*

I opened my mouth to explain, but where do you even start? "Brody—"

Eric didn't wait for me to finish. "Hey, brother. What's going on?" he said, grabbing Brody's arm with the kind of firmness that said, "I'm here, but don't test me."

"Leave me alone, okay? Let me figure this out," Brody snapped, shaking Eric off like a wet dog. He looked… rough. Like he'd been through the emotional wringer and forgotten to come out the other side. I mean, we all knew Lexi came with baggage, but Brody looked like he'd been hit by the entire luggage carousel.

Eric shot me a look, his brow furrowed in confusion, but he caught on fast. Felicia and I were out of our depth—this was Eric's time to shine. Brody took a step forward, but Eric was already there, positioning himself between Brody and the counter like a human shield. I felt a flicker of relief, but the air still felt charged, like the calm before a storm.

And then, as if the universe had a flair for drama, the door jingled again.

Lexi walked in, still in her scrubs, her face as unreadable as a crossword puzzle in a language I didn't speak.

"Lexi, I don't know what's happening," I said, my voice a mix of relief and panic as she stormed in like a hurricane in Crocs.

"Nothing is happening. *Right, Brody?*" Her tone was ice-cold, and I'd seen Lexi mad before, but this was next-level. She marched up to him and slapped the phone out of his hand like she was swatting a fly. "I said you're not doing anything, and that's fucking that. Do you understand me?"

Eric took a step back, giving Lexi space, and I crept out from behind the counter to stand beside him. Eric wouldn't lay a finger on Lexi—he wasn't that guy—but I was ready to step in if things escalated. Being this close to Brody was terrifying, but knowing Eric had my back made it slightly less so.

And cue the butterflies.

It was at that inopportune moment that I thought, *Why does Eric have to smell so good? Cologne or pheromones?*

"I'm doing it, Lexi," Brody said, his voice trembling with a mix of anger and desperation. "I'm tired of lying. I'm tired of pretending I'm nothing to you. I'm sick of this. Either you tell that old bastard you're done with him, or I'll make a video right now and blow it up. Just like Eric's. I swear I'll do it!"

Lexi laughed—a deep, throaty laugh that sent chills down

my spine. "Charles knows about you, you dingbat! Do you think I'm a fucking idiot? Do you think I'd risk everything I've worked for? You have no idea who I am, and that's how it'll always be. You're not up to par. Accept it, because it's never going to change."

Brody's face crumpled, his voice cracking as he shot back, "No, Lexi, you're the one who's always pretending. You pretend you don't love me. You pretend money's more important. But it's not true. It's not real. *We are.* That's the only real thing you have, and you know it deep down. You're the one who doesn't know who you really are. And that's the honest truth."

Brody was close to tears now, his voice cracking like a teenager's mid-puberty. "I may not know much, but I know this—if you don't leave him, you're never going to be loved like I love you ever again. I can't keep playing your game."

Lexi's expression didn't waver. "It's not a game. How many times do I have to tell you? I know what I'm doing, and I know what I want. And it's not you."

(Translation: *You're not even in the running, buddy.*)

"I swear I'll have money one day," Brody said, his voice trembling with a mix of defiance and desperation. "More than that old fossil probably has."

"But you don't *now*, do you?" Lexi shot back, her tone

sharper than a sushi chef's knife.

"But I will. Trust that. Trust *me*."

Lexi sighed, pinching the bridge of her nose. "Fucking hell, Brody! It wasn't about money with you, but you've made it impossible to enjoy any of this. You've ruined everything."

"Fine," Brody snapped, his voice cracking. "Go be with an old fart who needs Viagra just because he's got a trust fund. I'm done. I swear."

"Good," Lexi said, her voice icy. "Because we're through."

"Yeah," Brody said, wiping tears from his eyes with the back of his hand. "Yeah, we are."

Eric shifted uncomfortably next to me, and I dared to glance up at him. He gave me an apologetic look before stepping forward. "Let's leave the ladies in peace, okay?"

Brody hesitated, grumbling under his breath, but eventually gave in. As he walked past Lexi, he stopped and said, "I mean it. I'm done."

"I never want to see you again," she replied, her voice as cold as a January morning in Alaska.

The men walked out, and I finally let out the breath I'd been holding. "What the hell was that, Lexi?"

"It was nothing," she said, but the anger and pain etched on her face told a different story. "Just a mistake."

"That was very scary," Felicia chimed in, and I nodded in agreement.

"Yeah, well, it's over now," Lexi said, crossing her arms. "This is why I don't do this shit. I knew better, and I still went for it anyway."

"He fell in love," I said softly.

Lexi turned to me, her eyes blazing. "That is *not* love, Eva."

The door jingled open again, and Shane strolled in, looking as clueless as ever. "Sorry I'm late, Felicia—Jesus, did someone die or something? I'm like fifteen minutes late, jeez."

"Shane, you don't know the drama you just missed," Felicia said, dragging him toward the back room.

I turned back to Lexi. "What will you do now?"

"What I always do," she said, her voice steely. "I'll keep going until I get exactly what I want. Fuck Brody. Fuck Tegan. Fuck Charles. I'm done being nice to everybody."

With that, she pushed past me, flung the door open, and stormed out, leaving me standing there with a half-eaten tart and a whole lot of questions.

CHAPTER

FOURTEEN

THE SUN WAS CLINGING to the horizon like that one guest who overstays their welcome at a party, painting the desert in shades of "cotton candy pink" and "existential crisis purple." Across the valley, the Strip's neon lights winked at the dusk like a tipsy flirty aunt. I wondered if anyone else noticed how the desert and the city low-key hated each other but still showed up to the same reunion every night. Or maybe it was more like yin yang.

Cali fidgeted with a string of patio lights, her voice tentative. "Do you think Lexi's coming?"

I'd spent an hour arranging charcuterie boards artfully enough to impress a TikTok foodie, but now the cheese sweated under the fading light like it knew the truth: She's not coming.

"I hope so," I replied, sipping my drink. The unspoken hung heavier than Cali's rosemary-infused olive oil dip. Lexi had ghosted us harder than my ex after I mentioned The Incident. The Brody Incident, that is.

Cali sighed. "Claire's out too. Still recovering from the C-section."

"Maybe it's just us," I said, though the thought made my eye twitch. Girls' night without Claire's chaotic energy and Lexi's scandalous updates felt like a Netflix party watching paint dry.

"What about Morgan?" Cali asked, perking up.

I nearly choked on an overpriced olive. "Morgan? The human equivalent of a parking ticket? Hard pass."

(Lexi hadn't been wrong about Morgan's "don't talk to me" vibe. Claire's return can't come soon enough.)

Felicia swept in then, her presence as comforting as a weighted blanket. "Are we the only ones here?" she asked, eyeing the sad platter of untouched brie.

The desert breeze carried the scent of jasmine and unspoken drama. Somewhere, Tegan was probably Instagramming her *happily ever after* while Scott's family lawyers sharpened their knives. Lexi was… wherever Lexi was. And us? We had tequila, half-hearted gossip, and the kind of silence that begged for a confession.

"I think so," I said, clutching a margarita that was 80% tequila, 20% existential dread. I sighed, staring mournfully at the empty chairs where Claire and Lexi should've been. Our girls' night circle now resembled a sad game of musical chairs.

Felicia thrust a shot glass of murky liquid under my nose. "Try this. It's a spicy tamarind tequila fusion. I'm calling it Party in a Glass."

I sipped. It tasted like a fire alarm. "Wow. This could double as industrial paint stripper."

"Perfect," she said, unfazed. "Cali, prepare yourself. Tegan's wedding was a disaster. The centerpieces looked like they were assembled by a toddler on a sugar crash, and the cake? *Store-bought.*"

Cali gasped, nearly spilling her sparkling water. "Not *store-bought.*"

"Oh yes," Felicia chimed in, slamming back her tamarind tequila like a cowboy in a rom-com. "Lexi said the florist showed up with daisies. *Daisies*, Cali. Tegan's hashtag was literally *#OldMoneyVibes.*"

Just then, Lexi burst in like a hurricane in designer heels, her hair windswept in that I-just-left-a-scandal way. "Babes, sorry I'm late! Charles tried to guilt-trip me into a 'quiet night in'—as if I'd miss this dumpster fire debrief." She air-kissed Cali's baby bump. "How's my future godchild?"

Cali hugged her, beaming. "You came!"

"Of course! Now, where's the tequila? I need to catch up before Eva starts trauma-dumping about Eric again."

(Rude. But fair.)

As we dissected Tegan's wedding of shame (or *poors*, rather), Cali's eyes gleamed with the quiet vengeance of someone who'd once watched Tegan steal my prom date *and* my dignity. "Karma's a billionaire's messy divorce," she muttered.

"TBD," Felicia chirped in, too into her tamarind tequila to really care.

"Fitting," Cali said. "You know what they say about third generation wealth, 'shirtsleeves to shirtsleeves in three generations.'"

I blinked. "Is that… a laundry tip?"

"No, you heathen," Lexi said, rolling her eyes. "It means the Vanderbilts went from yachts to yard sales in a century. Old money isn't forever, haven't you seen *Downton Abbey*? Unless you're Charles, of course." She paused, smirking. "Fourth-gen. His trust fund could survive the apocalypse."

Felicia snorted. "Explains the wedding. If Scott's trust fund's drier than a gluten-free brownie, no wonder it looked like they hired a taxidermist to do the floral arrangements."

I clutched my marg like a lifeline. "Or maybe Tegan's just rebranding. You know, like when influencers stage 'rustic' weddings in a parking lot but call it 'curated urban decay'?"

Lexi arched a brow. "Puh-lease. Her Instagram's so filtered, I'm surprised her eyebrows haven't dissolved into the ether. Here—" She yanked her phone from her purse. "Behold! Tegan 2.0: BrideBot Edition."

We crowded around, gasping at photos of a venue that resembled Felicia's cousin's wedding—and she wasn't a yacht owner, either. "Wait," I said, squinting. "Is that her waist? Or did she Photoshop herself a corset made of lies?"

Cali, ever the voice of reason. "Be nice, Eva. It's not her fault she needs filters to look good IRL. Let's look at her Insta." She gasped. "That bitch blocked me."

Felicia said, "Same."

"Same," I said, a bubble laugh escaping. "Long ago."

Lexi rolled her eyes. "Amateurs. That's is why you keep a burner. Now, look—" She zoomed in on Tegan's "honeymoon" pic, where Scott glowed like a man who'd never paid taxes, green screen in full effect being him.

"Paradise? More like Photoshop Island. That palm tree is 70% clip art."

Felicia sighed, half-envious. "Where even is that? PNG Tropics?"

I snorted. "Her living room. She rented a green screen and a coconut, Scott included."

We burst into laughter, but beneath the giggles lurked the unspoken truth. We were all a bit jealous—if it were real, at least.

Lexi leaned back, her margarita sloshing dangerously close to the rim. "Tegan, cut the crap!" She yelled to her phone. "Her 'Nobu Villa' honeymoon is pure fiction. They've been squatting at the Wynn Villa for ages. You know, the one with all the charm of a airport lounge and an assisted living facility? Charles spilled it mid-wedding chaos."

Lingering jealousy lighting me up, I added, "Apparently, Scott's never even sniffed the Nobu bedsheets, not with Tegan, at least. Heather camped out there three days when Tegan was supposed to be living there. It's all lies and more lies with that one."

Lexi continued, "It's true! If Tegan were legit, she'd be gliding around the Bellagio Chanel, not the Wynn's."

I gasped, nearly inhaling a lime wedge. "The Bellagio

Chanel! Of course!"

(Translation: Why didn't I think of this earlier? Oh, yes. Because I didn't have every Chanel store memorized and itemized like it's the periodic table of handbags.)

(Side note: If my brain were a filing cabinet, the "Luxury Brands" folder would be labeled "Dreams I Can't Afford.")

(I.e.: Seven-year-old gaudy green car.)

Felicia squinted, her skepticism sharp enough to slice through Tegan's lies. "So Scott's not bankrupt? Are you quite sure?" There may or may not have been a slight hint of hope in her voice.

Lexi waved a hand, her nails glinting like tiny warning signs. "Please. Charles insists Scott's still rolling in it. Said if Scott ever got a job, they'd have nothing to talk about except the weather—and Charles thinks meteorology is for peasants." She paused to roll her eyes. "TFMAMs, am I right? I'm etching it onto his monogrammed towels, only I'm telling him it means That Fancy Man About Town."

I snorted. "You're diabolical."

Lexi shrugged. "He'll never find out."

The room fizzed with laughter until Cali, ever the human wrench in our gossip machine, blurted, "But what about Brody? The guy who looks like he bench press Charles with you on top?"

Lexi's smile evaporated faster than vodka at a bridal shower. "Let's just say Brody's… out. You wouldn't get it."

Cali crossed her arms. "Try me. I'm carrying a human. I can handle boy drama."

Felicia chimed in, "Lexi, the man has the emotional intelligence of an ant. What'd you expect—a knitting circle?"

Lexi groaned. "He showed up at the café, okay? Wanted to 'talk things through.' Next thing I know, he's talking about rearranging Charles' face with his fist. *Metaphorically*. Mostly. Nothing happened."

I chimed in. "But it could have."

Lexi leaned back, her margarita perched in one hand like a weapon. "He didn't do anything," she said, her voice as cool as the ice in her glass.

Unable to resist, I repeated, "But he *could* have."

Lexi groaned. "Look, I told Brody repeatedly—we were just having fun. Friends with *very specific* benefits. I even gave him the whole speech. 'Don't catch feelings, I'm not on that wavelength, blah blah blah.' If he didn't listen, that's his problem. I don't deal in *potential*—I deal in *bank accounts*. Real. Solid. Gold bank accounts. And if he couldn't grasp that, well…" She trailed off, her tone icy but with the faintest crack in her armor.

I leaned in. "And what about you? Did you catch feelings?"

She scoffed, ice queen. "Not for a second."

(Note: Her eyes flickered. Liar, liar, Prada on fire.)

Not convinced, I pressed further. "So… you're over him now?"

She took a long, dramatic sip of her drink. "Absolutely. I'm strictly a gold digger now. Fun's over. Time to focus."

Cali, who'd been watching and listening intently said, "Lexi, money isn't everything. You can be happy without a trust fund."

Lexi raised an eyebrow. "Says the woman married to a man who owns his own dental practice."

Cali shrugged. "Fair. But still."

The room fell silent, the clink of ice in our glasses the only sound. Beneath the banter, there was so much unsaid. Lexi's cool exterior was impressive, but I knew it was just a shield. A very expensive, designer shield.

Lexi went quiet, her eyes locked on Cali like she was trying to decode a secret message written in eyeliner. For a moment, the room felt heavy, like the air before a thunderstorm. I could almost see the ghosts of Lexi's past hovering around her—her mom stripping to pay the bills, her sisters following the same worn-out path. Lexi had always been determined to break the cycle, even if it meant trading love for Louis Vuitton.

Finally, she broke the silence, her voice sharp enough to cut glass. "I can love Charles *and* his trust fund. Not everyone dreams of marrying a dentist and moving to the suburbs to argue over lawnmowers."

(Translation: I'd rather cry in a Bentley than laugh in a minivan.)

There was something fierce in her words, like she was daring anyone to judge her. Love, in Lexi's world, was just another gamble she wasn't willing to take.

Before the mood could get any heavier, Felicia swooped in like a gossipy superhero. "Eva, don't think I didn't notice you rubbing on Eric at the café the other day," she said, her voice dripping with scandal.

I choked on my drink. "I did not!"

"Oh, please." Felicia grinned like the Cheshire Cat. "You leaned into him like he was a human space heater. Admit it —you were melting."

Cali joined in. "What does he even smell like? Spill."

I crossed my arms, feeling the burn on mu cheeks, and not from the tamarind tequila, either. "I didn't rub on him!"

The teasing spiraled, and I couldn't help but laugh. There was something oddly comforting about the memory of Eric's cologne lingering in the air, even if it was just for a second. Maybe it was the alcohol, or maybe it was the way the night felt like a warm hug, but for a moment, everything felt lighter.

As the laughter swirled around us, I caught myself smiling. Because sometimes, it's the little things—like the scent of a man you probably shouldn't like but *do*—that make life feel a little less complicated.

CHAPTER

FIFTEEN

"MORGAN IS SATAN'S RECEPTIONIST," Lexi declared. "I swear, she's got a PhD in Passive Aggressive Post-Its."

We'd crammed ourselves behind the office computer (which wheezed like an asthmatic grandpa) and a file cabinet that hadn't seen a label maker since 2013. Our "spy perch" offered a pristine view of Morgan's signature Resting Clipboard Face at the front desk.

"What fresh hell did she unleash today?" I whispered, though I wasn't worried about being overheard. The entire staff hated Morgan so much, even the stapler seemed to side-eye her.

Lexi snorted. "She told me nurses aren't allowed to 'loiter' at reception. *Loiter!* As if I'm a teenager hanging outside a 7-Eleven! Then she said I was 'making her nervous.'"

I shook my head. "Think she knows Claire's water broke right where she's sitting? Imagine if we told her that office chair is a *birth canal memorial*."

Lexi's grin turned wicked. "She'd faint. Or quit. Or faint *while* quitting. Either way, confetti."

"I miss Claire," I sighed. "She never policed our loitering. Or our snack drawer."

"Claire's a saint. Morgan's a piece of work."

I tried to focus on my patient notes, but my brain was too busy replaying The Brody Incident at the café—specifically, the moment Eric's calloused fighter's hand brushed mine.

(Cue internal panic: Was that accidental? Intentional? A secret Morse code for "I like you"?)

Lexi jabbed my arm. "Earth to Eva. You're doing that thing again."

"What thing?"

"The 'I'm mentally slow-dancing with Eric in a rainstorm' thing. It's nauseating."

"I am not—"

"You are. And FYI, he's got a girlfriend. A Buff Barbie named… Marcy. Or Darcey? Something that sounds like a candle scent."

Misty Mindy, actually, not that I cared.

"I'm not thinking about Eric!"

"Liar. Your pupils just dilated like you've seen a photo of his dick."

Before I could protest, Morgan's voice sliced through the air. "Ladies? *Lingering* again?"

Lexi muttered, "Act natural," before grabbing a chart and announcing, "Just discussing patient care protocols, boss!" She rolled her eyes again and said, "What is it, then?"

"Oh, you know, just casually freaking out about Eric's fight tomorrow," I said, waving a hand like I was swatting a gnat and not my own spiraling anxiety. "VIP tickets! So glamorous! Unless I trip and spill nachos all over myself. Which I will."

Why did I say yes? I thought, *why do VIP tickets feel like a subpoena?*

Lexi squinted at me, her expression a mix of pity and delight. "Why, do you need an outfit? Something that screams 'I'm chill and I've definitely not thought about that dick print on my—'"

"Lexi!"

She laughed. "Oh, come on. Let's raid my closet. I've got a sequined tube top that says 'funeral appropriate' if you squint."

"It's not about the outfit," I lied, already mentally vetoing my entire wardrobe.

"Liar. You're nervous seeing him in all his professional fighter state will do naughty things to your dreams."

"I am not," I said, but she wasn't totally wrong.

"Or are you scared he'll bring Misty Mindy along and swipe those VIP tickets from you and give them to her?" Lexi said, rolling her eyes. "Relax. If she clings to him like a koala again, I'll accidentally not on accident spill my drink on her."

"Lexi, no—"

"Lexi, *yes*," she countered, grinning. "Charles is being a brat about Brody, but I'll guilt him into taking me. 'Darling, if you don't go, I'll have to flirt with the ring announcer.' Works every time."

I groaned. "You two are like *Succession* meets *The Bachelor—The Golden Bachelor*. It's exhausting."

"And yet, fascinating," she said. "Now, about this fight. You're overthinking. Eric's into you. That hand grab? Please. He's basically shouting 'I pick you!' in Morse code."

"He has a girlfriend, Lexi."

"Like that's ever stopped anyone!"

"She's buff, Lexi. She could bench-press me."

"Exactly! He needs you for conversation. And let's face it —you're way cuter in athleisure."

As Lexi prattled on about "strategic denim" and smoky eyes that say "I'm not into you, you're into me," I mentally drafted my exit plan. Step 1) Fake a sudden allergy to excitement. Step 2) Hide in a supply closet until— indefinitely.

But then she dropped the bomb: "We're picking outfits after work. And no, Eva, athleisure is not allowed."

I fled before she could suggest heels, my stomach churning like a washing machine full of regret. Because tomorrow, I'd either be the heroine of a rom-com… or the punchline of a meme.

⁓

My bedroom looked like a fashion crime scene. Clothes erupted from every corner—a volcanic spew of denim, polyester, and regret. Felicia, Lexi, and I stood amidst the chaos, surveying the damage like detectives at a Who Wore It Worst? convention.

Lexi held up a sequined top from 2016. "Eva, why did you wait until the literal night before to pick an outfit? This isn't a crisis; it's a war crime."

I admit I was defensive. "I thought my 'Cozy Librarian' cardigan vibe would work! It's Calvin Klein!"

Felicia grinned like she'd won a gold star. "My outfit's been ready for weeks. Lexi even approved it."

(Translation: I'm the Hermione of this group.)

Lexi tossed a floral romper into the "nope" pile (now taller than me). "This isn't a romper. It's a sack of despair. We're raiding my closet. Now."

Twenty minutes later, I stood in Lexi's condo—a penthouse so sleek, I half-expected a butler named Jeeves to offer me a champagne flute. The view alone could've paid my rent for a decade.

"This place is ridiculous," I breathed, staring out Lexi's floor-to-ceiling windows at the Strip glittering below like a disco ball someone dropped from space. My finest hotel stays suddenly felt like camping trips in comparison.

Lexi flicked a strand of hair with the drama of a shampoo

commercial, and shot me a look. "I've been hinting at Charles to upgrade me to a penthouse with a helipad, but he's too busy golfing with senators or whatever billionaires do." She vanished into her walk-in closet—a room bigger than my entire apartment, stocked with enough sequins to blind a disco—and emerged holding an outfit that screamed "Gold digger passing by!"

"Prepare to be transformed."

I side-eyed the slinky dress. "Lexi, I can't wear this. I'm built like a teapot—short and stout."

Lexi rolled her eyes. "Nonsense. This dress is magic. It's been to two galas and a yacht party. It'll make you look like a Bond girl who accidentally became a neuroscientist and is a double agent for whichever countries are fighting again."

As I wriggled into the dress (Note: Spanx are the devil's leggings), I couldn't help but marvel at Lexi's life. Marble countertops. A chandelier. A fridge stocked with multiple brands of sparkling water. How did she swing this with our salary?

(Answer: Charles. Always Charles.)

The dress fit, but I wasn't feeling it. "I don't know. It's a bit tight?"

"Fine. Wear this, then."

The second outfit Lexi pulled out of her closet was stunning, if you ignored the fact that it looked like it had been designed by a dominatrix who moonlighted as a fashion editor. Black jeans so tight they could've doubled as compression socks, and a leather top that screamed "FBI agent by day, rockstar by night." Not my usual vibe, but I tried it on anyway—and miracle of miracles—it fit. Lexi adjusted the hem with the precision of a neurosurgeon, then stepped back to admire her handiwork.

"See? You look amazing," she said, grinning. "You're welcome! Now, add gold hoops, those boots you've been hiding under your bed, and maybe a leather jacket—if it weren't hotter than Satan's armpit out there."

I opened my mouth to thank her, but she bulldozed on. "Also, contour your cheekbones. And never wear beige near me again. You're lucky we found something that doesn't make you look like a sentient potato sack."

Her phone rang, cutting off her *Project Runway* pep talk. "Unlisted?" she muttered, declining the call. It rang again. "Fucking Brody. He's like nonstop spam email. Eva, you were there when I told him to get lost, right?"

Before I could nod, it rang a third time. She answered, snapping, "What do you want?" A pause. "Of course I know it's you. Who else would call 17 times after being ghosted?

TMZ has better boundaries."

I seized the chance to escape, clutching my new dominatrix-chic ensemble. "Thanks, Lexi!" I whisper-yelled, backing toward the door.

She waved absently, still ranting at Brody, while I took one last look at her condo—a Pinterest board come to life—and fled.

"Felicia is going to die when I tell her about this," I announced to the empty elevator, which dinged cheerfully, oblivious to my existential crisis.

Later, curled in bed with a pint of ice cream, my phone buzzed.

Lexi: "Going to the fight after all. See you there."

(Translation: She'd made up with Brody.)

Because of course she had. Drama was Lexi's cardio.

Perfect timing, really. I still had to survive Eric's fight, avoid Misty Mindy's biceps of doom, and pretend I hadn't accidentally become internet famous for calling Eric a "disgusting pig."

CHAPTER

SIXTEEN

THE T-MOBILE ARENA THROBBED like a nightclub that had swallowed three Red Bulls. Felicia and I shuffled inside, elbows tucked in, navigating a minefield of rowdy, beer-swilling fans. Honestly, the pre-fight hype was intense. I half-expected someone to start auctioning off Eric's sweaty hand wraps.

(Note to self: If they do, *do not bid*. Even if it's for charity. *Especially* if it's for charity.)

"We're early!" Felicia chirped, as if that mattered. The place was already jammed with people shouting things like "Mann's gonna knock him out!" and "I bet fifty on a TKO!" Meanwhile, I was just here to survive the night without accidentally making eye contact with Eric's abs.

My hoop earrings had become my emotional support

accessories. *Twist. Adjust. Repeat.* If I fidgeted them enough, maybe I'd teleport to my couch. Felicia, of course, was thriving.

"You," she announced, spinning to face me, "look like a smoke-show. Lexi's closet deserves a Nobel Prize." She blew a chef's kiss, then added, "If I weren't morally opposed to leather, I'd steal that top."

"Look who's talking. You look like a Bond girl who moonlights as a pastry chef," I fired back. And she did—her apron-to-bodysuit glow-up was staggering. Lexi had somehow turned Felicia's "I knead dough at 5 a.m." vibe into "I casually own a vineyard."

We carved a path through the crowd—a *Lord of the Flies* meets *Jerry Maguire* situation—before collapsing into our seats. I slouched low, mentally drafting my disguise, Eva Incognito, Woman Who Definitely Didn't Go Viral That One Time.

Then Felicia's nails dug into my arm. "Holy. Shit."

I followed her stare.

Tegan.

Of course. Because why should tonight be simple? There she was, gliding through the crowd like a shark in a sequin dress. Scott trailed behind her, his Rolex glinting like a homing beacon. (TFMAM Alert: Trust Fund Middle-Aged *Money-pit*.)

On impulse, I waved. *Why?* Because once, at a club, I'd twerked to "Uptown Funk" in his face after three champagne coupes. Regret? Absolutely. But now we were bonded for life, Scott and I. He nodded back, looking vaguely amused.

Felicia snorted. "Remember when you said tonight would be low-key?"

"Once the lights are out, Fel. Give it some time."

The lights dimmed, the crowd roared, and the announcer bellowed Eric's name. My stomach did a backflip.

As Eric strode into the ring, all brooding intensity and biceps, the arena morphed into a stage for every messy, glittering drama we'd ever cooked up. Tegan's smirk, Felicia's glee, my existential earring crisis—it was *Real Housewives* meets *Rocky*, and we were all weirdly, terribly here for it.

Felicia leaned over, grinning. "Ten bucks says Tegan's here to scout alimony lawyers."

"Twenty says she already has one on speed dial," I whispered back.

Tegan looked like she'd just bitten into a lemon stuffed with wasps. I, meanwhile, fought to keep my smile from morphing into a full-blown evil cackle.

"You're deranged," Felicia hissed, though her shoulders shook with suppressed laughter. It'd been weeks since we'd squared off with Tegan Anderson, and honestly? The drama was delicious. Like finding out your high school bully now sells pyramid scheme leggings. Or maybe it was the fighting electricity crackling in the air.

"She's got the nerve of a telemarketer," I muttered, eyeing Tegan's sequined dress—a look I'd call "Pageant Mom Gone Rogue."

"At least our seats are better," Felicia chirped, waving her VIP lanyard like it was a golden ticket.

Then, like a horror movie jump-scare, "Eva!" Tegan's voice sliced through the crowd, sugar-coated and lethal. She waved like a wind-up doll possessed by a demon.

I turned, grudgingly, to find Scott slumped beside her, scrolling his phone with the enthusiasm of a man watching paint dry.

"Darling!" Tegan trilled. "Isn't the VIP section divine? I'm so glad you finally got to experience it. Must feel like Cinderella after the ball, hm?"

I looked back to her seats, grinned sweetly. "Funny, I was just thinking the same about your seats. Third row? Did Scott's trust fund bounce, or does Eric just hate you that much?"

Felicia choked on her rum and Coke. Tegan's smile froze, her Botox trembling.

Before she could retort, Lexi materialized beside us, dressed in what I can only describe as "Assassin Chic"—a black crop top, an oversized blazer, and boots that screamed "I'll step on you, and you'll like it." Brody trailed her like a lost puppy, all brooding muscles and regret.

"Ladies," Lexi purred, sliding into her seat. "Are we bullying Tegan, or is this a solo mission?"

Tegan's eye twitched. "Charming as ever, Lexi."

"I try," Lexi said, winking. "But let's be real—you're here for the free champagne, and we're here to watch Eric punch someone. Priorities, darling."

As the lights dimmed a tad more, I stole a glance at Brody. He was staring at Lexi like she'd invented electricity. (Question: Is it love, lust, or Stockholm syndrome? Jury's out.)

Charles wasn't exactly winning "Boyfriend of the Year" either. The man was a walking TFMAM cliché—sprinkling cash like human confetti while treating Lexi like a Lamborghini he could lease, crash, and replace. But Lexi? She treated his antics like a tax write-off for her soul, shrugging off his nonsense with the grace of a queen tolerating a jester.

(Translation: Between Brody and Charles, they made up one man. *Kidding!* I guess.)

Tegan, two rows back, piped up like a GPS set to Passive Aggressive. "Lexi! Charles will hear about this," she sing-songed, waving at Brody like she'd caught Lexi smuggling a penguin into a sauna.

Lexi, without missing a beat, said, "Tell him I said hi—and while you're at it, tell him to buy me that diamond necklace I sent him. The one shaped like a middle finger." She flipped Tegan an actual middle finger for emphasis, then spun back around, leaving Tegan gaping like a goldfish out of water.

Tegan scrambled for her phone, probably to document this scandal for her "I'm telling Charles" story. But Lexi, ever the drama queen, yanked Brody's collar and planted a kiss on him so intense, it could've been rated NC-17.

It was official. Tegan had no idea who she was dealing with. Lexi's "bag" wasn't a purse—it was a black hole where men's common sense went to die. Charles Rich? Just her latest shiny toy. Rumor had it he'd been waffling on the prenup, unlike Scott, who'd married Tegan faster than you can say "split assets." But Lexi played Charles like a kazoo—

letting him dangle promises like carrot sticks while she racked up designer carrots and Brody-sized biceps.

As the lights dimmed, I relaxed into my seat, smugly savoring the AC blasting my VIP-section sweat away. But then—*oh, universe, you little troll*—the Jumbotron lit up with... *my face.*

(Translation: The Viral Video.)

There I was, angry-yelling at none other than the night's hero—Eric.

Felicia, choking on laughter, said "Eva! You're famous!"

My heart did a backflip, then promptly filed for bankruptcy. I sank into my seat, wishing I could spontaneously combust or, at the very least, be swallowed by a conveniently timed sinkhole. The arena was dark, thank god, because if anyone could see my face right now, they'd mistake it for a tomato that had just been told it was ready for pasta sauce.

The video played on, Eric's voice booming, "Tegan has never, nor will she ever be my girlfriend." Each word felt like a public strip tease of my dignity.

I peeked two rows over. Scott was muttering to Tegan, his face redder than a lobster in a tanning bed. Even the TFMAM wasn't immune to viral embarrassment.

Then the screen shifted, the announcer roared Eric's name, and the crowd erupted when he introduced Eric Mann as the night's headliner. Lexi had been right—his rise to fame was fueled by that cursed video. I should've felt a flicker of pride for my accidental role in his success. Instead, I felt like a goldfish that had been flushed down the toilet and was now watching its life story on Netflix.

Then, as if the universe hadn't humiliated me enough, "Misty" Mindy Jones appeared on the big screen. She was training, all muscles and menace, like a superhero who skipped the cape and went straight for the "I'll destroy you" vibe. I felt a weird mix of awe and envy. Go her. Meanwhile, I was over here trying to remember how to breathe without sounding like a dying walrus.

Lexi caught my eye and smirked. "Ready to rumble, Cinderella?"

"Born ready," I lied, straightening my top.

The lights came up, and the emcee's voice boomed, "And here she is—the girl from the viral video!"

The camera panned to me. I froze, my smile so forced it could've cracked porcelain.

Lexi snapped her fingers. "Eva! Sit up straight, smile, and pretend you're having the time of your life. Fake it till you make it, baby."

I sat up, channeling my inner Hollywood Starlet Who Definitely Didn't Just Panic-Sweat Through Her Leather Top. I smiled. I laughed. I flipped my hair like I was auditioning for a shampoo commercial. If they wanted a performance, I'd give them one.

(Translation: What choice did I have?)

But beneath the glitter and forced cheer, one thought burned.

Eric Mann, you're a dead man.

CHAPTER

SEVENTEEN

IF YOU'VE EVER WONDERED how long a fight lasts, let me save you the suspense: *forever*. Or, more accurately, long enough to make you question every life choice that led you to this moment. I'd naively imagined Eric swaggering into the ring, throwing a few punches, and then bowing out like a rockstar. Instead, I got *UFC: The Extended Director's Cut*, complete with undercard fights, dramatic entrances, and Brody's running commentary.

"I should be in there," Brody grumbled, flexing like he was auditioning for a protein shake commercial. "I'm closer to Eric's weight class than these guys."

I thought, *Closer to his weight class or closer to his ego? Jury's out.*

By the time the second fight ended, I was ready to

scream. "I'm going to the bathroom," I announced, desperate for a break from the camera pans and Brody's "I'm basically a fighter too" monologues.

Lexi sprang up, tired of sitting. "I'll come with you."

Felicia grabbed her bag. "Same. This is the most action I've gotten all night."

The bathroom became our sanctuary—a fluorescent-lit haven of whispered grievances and lipstick touch-ups.

Lexi, glaring at her reflection, said, "I can't stand Brody. He's like a human mosquito—buzzing in your ear, impossible to swat away."

Felicia tried to lighten the mood. "At least he's keeping us entertained."

"Entertained?" Lexi said, reapplying her lipstick with the precision of a surgeon. "He's lying through his teeth. He's not fighting tonight because, A) he's not Eric, and B) he's about as skilled as a toddler in a bouncy castle."

I leaned against the sink, tired of it all. "Well, at least he's not using you for clout."

The words slipped out before I could stop them. Lexi froze, her lipstick hovering mid-air.

"True. But honestly, I miss Charles. At least he was

upfront about being a TFMAM. Brody's just… exhausting."

Angry, I muttered, "Eric could've warned me about the video. I feel like I'm starring in a reality show I never auditioned for."

Felicia patted my arm. "Welcome to the club. At least you're trending."

"Trending?" I groaned? "I'm a *meme*. A cautionary tale. A 'what not to do at a UFC fight' PSA."

"I can't believe this is happening again," Felicia hissed, her face scrunched up like she'd just bitten into a lemon. "If the café fills up with Eric Mann groupies one more time, I'm quitting and opening a bakery in Antarctica."

"Same," I groaned, remembering the Great Raspberry Tart Famine.

Lexi, meanwhile, was busy perfecting her reflection in the mirror, flicking her hair this way and that. "Relax, you two. This whole circus is amazing for my follower count. Everyone associates me with the video now—not you guys."

"It's not your face on the Jumbotron," I grumbled.

"At least you look stunning, Eva," Felicia said, patting my arm like I was a prize poodle. "Like, next-level stunning. You're basically a walking filter."

"I do look good," I admitted, glancing at my reflection.

The leather top and gold hoops were working overtime. "But these earrings are trying to murder me. They're so heavy, I'm surprised my earlobes haven't filed for divorce."

Lexi rolled her eyes. "Don't you dare take them off. You'll ruin the whole vibe." She rummaged through her designer purse and pulled out a bandaid. "Here. Stick this behind your ear. It'll help."

I watched in awe as she bit the bandaid into shape. "Is this a stripper hack? A spy trick? What are you?"

She tucked the bandaid behind my ear with surgical precision. "A genius. Now stop whining."

Miraculously, the earrings felt lighter.

"Next, she'll teach us how to turn duct tape into a clutch," Felicia said with a sly smirk.

Just then, Tegan waltzed into the bathroom like she owned the place. We all turned our backs in unison—a silent "You're dead to us" that spoke volumes.

"Girls, let's go!" someone called, and we filed out, leaving Tegan to stew in her own irrelevance.

Back in our seats, the next fight was underway. Misty Mindy vs. Deadly Wendy. Wendy was tall, lean, and looked like she could bench-press a Prius. She landed a kick that sent Mindy sprawling, but Mindy rallied with a punch that could've knocked out a grizzly bear. By the end of the round, both fighters were bleeding, and the crowd was roaring.

Felicia winced. "This is like *Mean Girls*, but with more blood."

I nodded, scared all of a sudden. "And fewer apologies. There's no way I'm provoking Mindy," I muttered under my breath, plastering on a neutral expression that screamed "I'm totally fine, nothing to see here." I'd learned my lesson. Mindy's anger was like a hurricane with a gym membership—best avoided. Still, I mentally rehearsed my post-fight script, "Great job, Mindy! You and Eric are couple goals!"

(Translation: Please don't punch me.)

Then the bell rang, and Mindy went full Tasmanian Devil. In less than two minutes, she turned Deadly Wendy into a human pretzel, twisting her arms and landing punches so savage, I half-expected Wendy to start crying for her mom. The ref had to check if she was still conscious before calling it.

"Holy crap," I whispered.

"She's like a ninja. A very angry ninja," Felicia said, eyes wide.

Lexi smirked. "I'd pay to see her fight Tegan."

Then the lights dimmed, and Eric's entrance began. His

team marched in with black and white flags that read "Eric 'The Terror' Mann."

I giggled, nervously. "The Terror? Since when?"

"Since he realized 'Eric 'The Guy Who Drinks Great Coffee' Mann' doesn't sell tickets," Felicia said.

The rival team entered next, waving green flags for Joey "Scrappy" Carrano—the reigning champ and crowd favorite. Eric, the underdog who'd landed this fight thanks to our viral video, now had everything to prove.

The bell rang, and Eric transformed. Gone was the guy who'd awkwardly brushed my hand at the café. In his place was a machine—every punch, every dodge executed with surgical precision.

Then Scrappy tackled him, slamming him into the cage so hard, I felt the vibrations in my teeth.

"Oh my god."

Felicia clutched my arm. "Is he okay?"

Please get up, please get up.

Unfazed, Lexi said, "Relax. He's fine. Probably."

The camera swung to me, and suddenly my face was plastered on the big screen like I'd accidentally wandered into a reality TV show. Normally, I'd be mortified—I avoid the spotlight like it's a swarm of wasps—but tonight? Tonight, I was too busy watching my own personal nightmare unfold.

Eric was down. *Way* down. The champion, Scrappy (which, honestly, sounds like a name you'd give a puppy, not a man who punches people for a living), was pummeling him like a piñata at a kid's birthday party. Blood, sweat, and what I hoped wasn't a tooth flew everywhere. And something inside me just snapped.

I shot to my feet, my voice shaking like a leaf in a hurricane. "Eric, get up!" I screamed.

"Holy fuck," Brody echoed beside me, his voice cracking like a teenager's. "Get up, Eric! If he loses this, he's done. Done."

Felicia grabbed my hand, her grip so tight I thought she might accidentally break it. The crowd was a blur of noise and motion, but all I could see was Eric, battered and bloody, struggling to his feet.

And then—like a scene straight out of a Rocky movie— Eric pushed Scrappy aside and mounted him with the kind of raw intensity that made the crowd lose their collective minds. The bell rang, and Eric staggered back to his corner, his face a mess of blood and swelling. One eye was practically shut, but the other locked onto mine with a fierceness that made my heart skip a beat.

I forced a smile—a wobbly, please-don't-die kind of smile —and he managed to grin back, despite looking like he'd just gone ten rounds with a blender. For a split second, everything felt almost… okay. That minute in between rounds felt like a second, a second where we locked eyes, his coach yelling things I couldn't hear, but I could see—and he was giving me a look that said "I got this I swear!"

The fight resumed, and Eric—battered, bruised, and looking like he'd been through a wood chipper—somehow found the strength to land a kick so brutal it made Joey's leg buckle like a folding chair. Then, with a punch that could've knocked out a small elephant, he sent the champion crashing to the floor. For good.

The arena erupted. Cheers, screams, and what sounded like someone blowing a vuvuzela filled the air. Eric Mann, the underdog who'd gone viral for all the wrong reasons, had just become a champion.

And then, like a scene from my worst nightmare, a reporter materialized out of nowhere, shoving a microphone in my face. "How does it feel to have a boyfriend who's just won the UFC championship?" she demanded, her voice dripping with faux enthusiasm.

My heart did a backflip. I started to smile—because, honestly, who wouldn't?—but then my brain caught up. Wait.

Boyfriend?

"I am *not* his girlfriend," I blurted out, my voice sharper than a freshly sharpened pencil. Then, in a desperate attempt to redirect the chaos, I added, "Maybe ask Misty Mindy. She's the one you should be interviewing right now."

The reporter blinked, her face scrunching up like she'd just bitten into a lemon. "Misty Mindy? She won her fight tonight, but her girlfriend isn't a champion," she said slowly, as if explaining basic math to a toddler.

"*Girlfriend?*" I repeated, my brain short-circuiting.

"Well," the reporter said, gripping the microphone like it was a lifeline. "If you're not Eric's girlfriend, then who is?"

"Misty Mindy," I said, each word landing like a lead balloon.

The reporter stared at me like I'd just declared the moon was made of cheese. "Misty Mindy is not Eric's girlfriend. She's gay."

As the arena roared around me, I stood there, a human puddle of humiliation and disbelief.

Oh, fucking hell, I thought. *Not again.*

Please turn the page for a sneak peek

into Girl Fight Series book 3

SUMMER STORM

available now.

SUMMER STORM

Girl Fight Book 3

CHAPTER

ONE

SCORCHING.

Not "oh, isn't it a bit warm?" scorching. Not "maybe I'll fan myself with a napkin" scorching. No, this was *Satan's armpit hosting a Bikram yoga retreat* scorching. My car—a 2015 relic I've affectionately dubbed The Green Toaster—

was living up to its name. The AC wheezed like an asthmatic hamster on a Peloton, blowing air that felt like a hairdryer set to *apocalypse*. By the time I pulled into Desert Bloom Café, sweat was pooling in places I didn't even know *had* places.

Summer had barged in like an overzealous intern who'd mainlined six Red Bulls, and I was already drafting my resignation from The Mojave Desert, Inc., Summer Division. I yanked down the sun visor, which—thanks to my petite stature (i.e.: genetically cursed to be eye-level with steering wheels)—mostly framed the sky like a tragic art exhibit titled "The Sun: Yes, It's Still There."

"Fuuuucking visor," I hissed, sitting on the tiptoe of my ass like a meerkat with a caffeine deficiency. *Please, Felicia,* I mentally pleaded, *have my coffee ready. Make it cold enough to freeze hell.*

By the time I parked, my cleavage had evolved into a microclimate. A greenhouse under each *globe*.

(Note: Buy stock in baby powder.)

I lunged for the café door, yelping as the handle seared my palm like a forgotten panini press. "Jesus H. Christ!" I yelped, briefly considering suing the sun for emotional damages.

Inside, the AC hit me like the Antarctic ice wall. I

gasped, *alive again.*

"There you are," Felicia said, sliding over my cortado. "I added extra ice. You look like you wrestled a greased otter in a slip-'n-slide factory."

I grabbed the cup, downing it like a parched camel, wishing it was a Big Gulp instead. The caffeine hit my bloodstream like a motivational speaker on a sugar rush. *I am alive! I am powerful! I am… still sweating through my bra.*

I slumped into my usual seat, where the AC vent blew directly onto my forehead. Outside, the newly planted trees swayed smugly, sipping iced tea and laughing at my plight. "Show-offs," I muttered. But secretly, I admired their audacity. If a tree could thrive in Satan's armpit (i.e.: Vegas), maybe I could too. Or at least survive without being mistaken for a melted popsicle.

The heat had me daydreaming about truly rational life choices. Moving to Antarctica. Marinating in a kiddie pool of aloe vera. Trading my scrubs for a Yeti™-brand snowsuit. But then I remembered—I had a shower at home I planned to convert into a polar expedition. Arctic tundra vibes, here I come.

"How much longer?" I whined to Felicia, who looked about as ready to go as at the start of her shift.

"Ten minutes," she said, swatting the already clean

counter with a rag. "Unless you want to power-wash me with the espresso machine."

"I would," I sighed, "but Shane would be mad, probably."

My thoughts inevitably drifted to Eric Mann—the tall, dark, and infuriatingly handsome UFC fighter who gymmed two doors down and had turned my life into a rom-com meets action movie. There was something about him—like a human electromagnet in a leather jacket, pulling me into his orbit with the subtlety of a fireworks show.

It wasn't exactly a secret that I often played Felicia's Uber. Eric seemed to know it too. More than once, I'd caught him "casually" strolling toward the café just as I pulled up. Coincidence? Stalking? A secret side hustle as a parking lot influencer? I didn't ask questions.

After a parade of women had thrown themselves at him—including my ex-bestie, who stole my high school sweetheart like she was snatching the last pizza at a bridal shower—I'd finally let go of my crush. Our connection had mellowed into something friendlier, less "will they, won't they" and more "oh, hey, you're here again."

Still, I hadn't seen him in person since his first big fight—a night I attended in VIP, thank you very much—where I learned two things: 1) Blood is way louder in real life, and 2) Leather seats are a sweaty choice in May.

Instead, he'd slid into my DMs.

Of course, the fallout wasn't just about Eric. Everyone had seen my mortifying interview with Cheryl Marsh, the sports reporter who'd grilled me like I was the star of *Making a Murderer: UFC Edition*. I'd fallen for gossip again without fact-checking. *Dope!*

(Note: My life is basically a "What Not to Do" TikTok series sponsored by Regret™.)

Now, my name was trending again on social media—because why let a girl live in peace?—while Eric Mann was skyrocketing to fame like a rocket fueled by biceps and charisma. He'd been featured on podcasts, asked about those viral clips (you know, the ones where I accidentally became the internet's favorite hot mess), and somehow, I'd become the accidental muse to his rise. Think Shakespeare's muse, if Shakespeare's muse had tripped into a UFC ring.

I'd scrolled past meme after meme of The Misunderstanding: Fight Night Edition. There I was, forever frozen in pixelated shame "Eva's Guide to Viral Fame: Step 1) Yell at a Fighter. Step 2) Gossip?" Embarrassing? Sure. But at this point, my face was basically the poster child for "Oops, My Bad" moments. I'd leaned into the cringe like it was a yoga pose. *Namaste, humiliation, release.*

Eric, though? He had this way of talking about those

embarrassing moments—so soft, so gentle—that it somehow made the humiliation sting less. I'd listened to him on a few podcasts, stunned by how candid he was about that unfortunate journey. He thought kinder about me than I did of myself sometimes.

Maybe that's why my stomach did a full Olympic floor routine when his DM popped up post-fight. Backflips! Cartwheels! A perfect 10 from the Russian judge!

At first, he explained he'd be MIA from the café scene for a few weeks—he needed to heal and rest.

(Translation: "I got punched in the face 87 times, but let's call it 'self-care.'")

I didn't blame him. If I'd won a fight that looked like a blender set to "puree," I'd need a vacation too. But for Eric, a "vacation" meant nonstop promo shoots, sponsorships, and grinning through interviews like his jaw wasn't held together by duct tape and prayer.

Strange as it was, that fight stirred up feelings I'd buried under a mountain of denial and Target clearance-rack wine. I'd never felt so fiercely protective of someone I'd publicly roasted like a holiday turkey. But I kept my distance. I hadn't confessed a thing—would I ever? The way I'd treated him had torched any chance of a rom-com ending. Now, we were just friends—a safe, uncomplicated label that let me sip my cortados without diving into the café's potted ferns every time he walked in.

Felicia slammed the espresso machine shut. "I'm almost done. Shane's nearly here."

"The same Shane who showed up an hour late to Brody's meltdown?" The guy was late more often than not, but at least he made good coffee.

"That's the one. If he ever opens a café, I'm naming my firstborn after him. Late-a-Latte."

Once Shane finally stumbled in, looking like he'd wrestled a tumbleweed, we fled into the Vegas heat—a dry, oppressive monster that hugged you like a jealous ex—and braved the heat home. The drive had been fast, but brutal—like an episode of *Survivor, The Highlight Reel*.

Fanning herself with a napkin, Felicia started. "Have you heard about Tegan?"

I nearly tripped over my own resentment while slipping out of my too-hot Crocs. "Ugh. What now? Did she patent Photoshop Wedding, Inc.? Spot her at Gold Diggers Anonymous? Scott finally kick the bucket?"

Felicia rolled her eyes, slumping on the couch, her face tomato-red. "Worse. She's in hiding."

"Who cares!" I croaked. "It's her own doing. She's

alienated herself, so *who freaking cares.*"

Felicia leaning in, doing one of her "I found something I shouldn't't've." "Well, yeah, but I did a *casual* Google search —"

"Casual?" I interrupted. "Felicia, your 'casual' searches could uncover Area 51's Wi-Fi password."

She ignored me, continuing, "—and stumbled onto a Subreddit called 'Where's Tegan?' It's part true crime, part 'where is this influencer?' type thing."

I gave in with a dramatic sigh and plopped down beside her, letting the AC cool me down. "Well... is she... dead?"

"Jesus, Eva! She's just missing. *Allegedly.* The thread's got theories—you have to see it for yourself. It's mostly, 'Is she in hiding? Did she fake her death? Or—"

I cut her off again. "—did she finally get canceled for that photoshopped wedding where her waist was smaller than her emotional IQ?"

"Eva! This is serious!"

"Alright, alright!"

"Another theory thrown around is that she's missing."

I scoffed. "As in *Gone Girl* missing or—"

She leaned in, tone more serious than my yearly pap. "As

in 'Has Scott done *something* to her?' The thread's got receipts longer than the Food Network. Remember her 'cheap' wedding? Turns out the unedited photos Lexi sent us—the ones where the flowers looked like they'd been bought at a gas station—leaked. Now the internet's dragging her like a prom dress on a gravel road."

I winced, not buying it. "Okay, but Tegan thrives on drama. She'll spin this into a 'vulnerability journey' and sell scented candles called 'Resilience' by next week."

"Normally, I'd agree," Felicia said, lowering her voice like she was about to reveal the secret ingredient in Coca-Cola. "But there's a video of her and Scott screaming at each other at Eric's fight. And now… radio silence? The Subreddit thinks she's…"

"Dead?" I whispered, half-wishing (*oh, come on*), half-intrigued.

"Eva!" Felicia groaned. "Can you take this seriously?"

I blinked. "How sure are you she's not just on a second—or, let's be honest, a *real*—honeymoon?"

She shook her head, stubborn as a burro in the desert. "Someone would've spotted her already. Linked an IP address to a post or something. She's MIA, Eva."

I slumped back, trying to process. Tegan had everything

—a trust fund, a mansion, a husband who probably had a pulse. Why vanish?

"Unless…" I gasped, a wild theory forming. "What if she is pulling a *Gone Girl*?"

"Why would she—"

"Yes! Fake her own disappearance to reboot her brand! It's genius. Disturbing, but genius." I snapped my fingers, the idea taking root. "Or," I countered, "she finally realized no amount of Photoshop can fix Scott's personality and she's better off… disappearing?"

Felicia shook her head, her curls bouncing.

"What is it, then?"

"That's the bad part. The Subreddit thread thinks Tegan's *missing* missing."

Hi, reader! Thank you for reading my story. I loved getting to know Eva and friends and I hope you loved them too.

If you feel up to it, please sign up to my newsletter! I'm not a spammer, so if you get an email every once in a while when I'm updating on new releases or bonus chapters, then it's something!

Subsribe to Blair's Newsletter

As an indie author, reviews are our lifeline. Please leave a review (if you want to!) on Amazon, Goodreads, or The StoryGraph.

Thank you for supporting me! It means the world.

P.S. Drop a line if you want to be in my ARC Team! Email at: authorblairmonroy@gmail.com.

About the Author

Blair Monroy writes funny rom-coms with memorable characters who love hard and play hard. When not writing, she's hanging out by the pool with rosé in one hand and a book in the other.

Spring Blues is the second book in the Girl Fight series.

IG: @blairmonroyauthor

TikTok: @authorblairmonroy

Email: authorblairmonroy@gmail.com

Books by Blair Monroy

GIRL FIGHT SERIES

Girl Fight

Spring Blues

Summer Storm

UPCOMING BOOKS

Autumn Falling